Finally

BY WENDY MASS

SCHOLASTIC PRESS / NEW YORK

Copyright © 2010 by Wendy Mass. All rights reserved. Published by
Scholastic Press, an Imprint of Scholastic Inc., *Publishers since 1920.* ·
SCHOLASTIC, SCHOLASTIC PRESS, and associated logos are trademarks and/or registered trademarks of Scholastic Inc. · No part of this
publication may be reproduced, stored in a retrieval system, or transmit-
ted in any form or by any means, electronic, mechanical, photocopying,
recording, or otherwise, without written permission of the publisher.
For information regarding permission, write to Scholastic Inc., Attention: Permissions Department, 557 Broadway, New York, NY 10012. ·
Library of Congress Cataloging-in-Publication Data · Mass, Wendy,
1967– · Finally / by Wendy Mass.—1st ed. · p. cm. · Summary: After
her twelfth birthday, Rory checks off a list of things she is finally
allowed to do, but unexpected consequences interfere with her
involvement in the movie being filmed at her school, while a weird
prediction starts to make sense. · ISBN: 978-0-545-05242-9
(hardcover) · [1. Maturation (Psychology)—Fiction.   2. Schools—
Fiction.   3. Motion Pictures—Production and direction—Fiction.
4. Accidents—Fiction.   5. Family life—Fiction.   6. Birthdays—
Fiction.]   I. Title. · PZ7.M42355Fin 2010 · [Fic]—dc22 · 2009015474 ·
10 9 8 7 6 5 4 3   10 11 12 13 14 · Printed in the U.S.A. 40 · First
edition, March 2010 · The text type was set in ITC Esprit Book · Book
design by Lillie Mear

FOR ALLISON AND COLLEEN
AND OUR 888 ADVENTURES!

Chapter One

I'm a big wisher. I'll wish on anything. Shooting stars, stray eyelashes, dandelion tops, coins in fountains. Birthday candles (my own and other people's). Even when my glasses fog up. When I was younger, the wishes used to vary. A pony. A best friend. A new bike with streamers on the handles. A baby brother or sister. Some of these even came true (not the pony). But over the past year, every wish has been spent wishing I was twelve already, a date I've waited for my whole life and one that is only six weeks away. Looking back, I wish I had saved one of those wishes because, if I had, I wouldn't be stuck in this drainpipe right now.

Yes, *drainpipe*.

Here's how it happened. My day started out pretty normal. My sixth grade class went on yet another field trip to the Willow Falls Reservoir. We were standing on the shoreline, listening to the guide go on about water tables and filtration systems as if they were the most fascinating things in the world. The air smelled swampy, and my orange sneakers were slowly sinking into the muddy banks. I kept glancing over at the forest on the other side of the shoreline. It reminded me of the setting of a fairy tale, like the ones my mom used to read me before bed. So peaceful and pretty, and sort of mysterious. At any minute Hansel or Gretel might dart out from between the trees. An opportunity to slip away came courtesy of Rex Bueford, who thought it would be funny to jump into the water. And it *was* funny, for about a second, until the tour guide told us that now our drinking water would taste like Rex's sweat.

While our teacher yelled at Rex, and then at his friends for laughing, I slowly backed away. I kept going until I couldn't hear the group anymore and found myself among a cluster of sharply sweet-smelling evergreens. The needles cushioned the ground beneath my feet, and a blue jay twittered on a low branch. I breathed in deep, and held the sweet air in my lungs. If my parents let me out of their sight more, I probably wouldn't have felt the need to escape from the group, but that's not going to change until I turn twelve. I have a whole *list* of things I'll finally get to do when that day arrives.

As I stood alone in the woods, a delicious chill of anticipation ran through me, as it always did when I thought of my twelfth birthday. I leaned back against a large gray rock, intending on gazing at the puffy clouds and daydreaming about the Big Day.

The only problem? That large gray rock? Not a rock. What I thought was solid igneous rock, here on earth since the creation of the planet and therefore more than sturdy enough to support my weight, was, in fact, a rubber flap covering the opening of a narrow gray drainpipe. When I realized this, my arms and legs flailed wildly. But I couldn't catch my balance in time. I fell, butt-first, into the pipe and was instantly wedged in. I could still see out if I craned my neck up. My sneakers dangled mere inches from the ground, but it might as well have been a mile since I couldn't move.

"Can anyone hear me?" I called as loudly as I could. "I'm stuck! Anyone?" But my voice got carried away by the wind like it was no more than a whisper. My head filled with my grandmother's voice. *Well, this is a fine kettle of fish.*

So that's how I wound up in this predicament. It's been a full minute now, and I haven't managed to get unstuck. I look around in a vain attempt to find something — anything — to wish on. I consider yanking out an eyelash, but that's kinda gross and probably painful. Plus, I don't think the wish would count if I did it that way.

I'm able to move an arm just enough to adjust my glasses, which have fallen off one ear. Now I can assess my situation. The pipe doesn't currently have any water running through it, so that's one good thing. And I don't appear to be hurt. No obvious blood or broken bones. I'm usually pretty coordinated. I can walk a straight line while patting my nose and rubbing my stomach, which isn't as easy as it sounds. If I wasn't stuck here, I could do it right now.

If I had a cell phone, I could use the voice-activated feature to call for help. Mental Note: Remind parents (if I ever see them again) that I wouldn't be in this situation if they'd gotten me a phone when I'd asked. Or any of the sixty-three *other* times I've asked, even though I swore each time I wouldn't lose it no matter what they thought. When I turn twelve, getting a phone is at the top of my list.

I watch through the gaps in the evergreens as the tour guide ushers my classmates back into the main building. The time must have come for the video portion of our visit. We've all been here so many times we know that old video by heart. If anyone ever quizzed us on how water makes its journey from clouds to our kitchen faucets, we'd all ace it. Still, coming here is a better field trip than the Willow

Falls Historical Society, which, unless you're a fan of musty old furniture that makes you sneeze, is deadly boring.

The last people to disappear into the building are my teacher and Rex Bueford. No doubt she's keeping an eye on him so he can't cause further harm to our town's water supply. Apparently no one, not even my best friend, Annabelle, has noticed I'm missing. This doesn't surprise me. Except for my parents (who notice me *too* much), I sort of fade into whatever background I'm next to, like a chameleon. I'm familiar with the habits of the chameleon because my science teacher used to keep one in a cage on his desk along with a pregnant hamster. Then last month the hamster, who was supposed to teach us about the reproductive process or whatever, got extra hungry from growing baby hamsters inside it and ate the chameleon. Well, *half* of the chameleon. So maybe the chameleon isn't a good example, but seriously, whenever I show up late to the lunch table, my friends seem surprised that I haven't been there all along.

I wish I had a book with me, since clearly I have a lot of time on my hands. I always carry around one or two, but we had to leave our backpacks on the bus. Not that I'd be able to turn the pages even if I *did* have a book. I wonder briefly if this drainpipe might lead somewhere as exciting as Alice's rabbit hole or Lucy's wardrobe, but Wonderland and Narnia have about as much in common with Willow Falls as a duck has with, well, something really different from a duck.

I try to twist my shoulders in one more futile attempt to break free. Eventually I give up and close my eyes. My mind wanders to one of my favorite daydreams: me, blowing out the candles on my birthday cake. My hair is sleek and wavy, my lips a light glossy pink, skin glowing. In my daydreams I'm always much prettier (and smarter, funnier, and more popular). I also never fall into drainpipes.

The sun warming my cheeks is soothing. And I admit, missing out on watching that old video isn't exactly breaking me up. I'm sure my class wouldn't board the bus without me. A few minutes later, my cheeks cool for a second, and I realize a shadow has passed across my face. I open my eyes and squint into the glare surrounding a short, plump old woman with very white hair. I hadn't heard anyone approach. I recognize her as the old woman who had taken our tickets when we first arrived. She had welcomed us warmly, as though she was truly happy to have us visit. Now her expression is stern as she frowns down at me.

"What do you think you're doing?" she asks, hands on

her hips. Her lips quiver a bit as she speaks, though, and I get the distinct impression she's trying not to laugh.

I sigh, used to being falsely accused of wrongdoing by my naturally suspicious parents. "I fell." I attempt to shrug my shoulders, but they don't move. "And now I'm stuck," I add.

She purses her lips, walks around the side of the pipe, then returns, shaking her head. "What's your name?"

I'm momentarily distracted by how the duck-shaped birthmark on her cheek wiggles when she speaks. She clears her throat and asks again.

I snap my gaze away from her cheek. "Rory," I tell her. "Rory Swenson."

"Rory," she repeats, putting a slight trill on the first syllable, which makes it sound a lot more exotic than it is. "Isn't that a boy's name?"

"It can be either one," I explain, trying not to clench my teeth. There's actually a boy named Rory a grade ahead of me, who Annabelle and I refer to as "Boy Rory." He and I avoid eye contact when we pass in the hall. Annabelle always gets a good laugh out of watching my reaction when people question me about my name. With a name like hers, no one accuses *her* of being a boy. Girly name aside, her long shiny blond hair and pink lip gloss scream, "I'm a girl!" In contrast, my boring brown takes a lot of taming before it looks even halfway decent, and I'm not allowed to wear makeup yet. And sadly, my bod doesn't look much different than Boy Rory's.

The old woman tilts her head toward the building. "You're here with the class?"

"Yes. I got lost. . . . I mean, I sort of wandered away. And then, well . . ." I gesture around me. "*This* happened."

"I see," she says, thoughtful. "Sometimes the universe, it wants us to pause for a moment. To reflect on what's happening in our lives."

"It does?"

She steps forward, peering at me so closely I begin to squirm. Or I *would* squirm, if I could move even an inch.

"What do *you* need to reflect on, Rory Swenson?"

"Um, me?" I stammer. "I don't have much, you know, going on in my life right now. The last eleven years have been pretty slow."

"Perhaps," the old lady agrees. "But you have many things coming your way. And not much longer to wait."

"How do you —"

She holds up a hand. "You won't get what you want, Rory Swenson, until you see what you need."

I smile up at her in an attempt to prove she's not totally

freaking me out. "I've got that covered," I reply. "I have a list and everything. And it's full of things I need."

"Is that so?" she asks with a slight raise of one eyebrow.

I suddenly feel the need to defend my list. "Nothing unreasonable or anything. Just things everyone else in the sixth grade can do."

"Everyone?" she asks.

I nod firmly.

"Well, you're all set then."

"Yes," I say confidently. "I guess I am."

"Excellent," she says, then turns to leave.

My eyes widen. "Wait! Can you find someone to get me out of here?"

She turns back and smiles. Before I know it, she's grabbed hold of both my wrists and tugged me right out. It takes me a few seconds to process this. I glance from the pipe, to the ground under my feet, to the woman. Standing beside her, I see I have a few inches on her, and I'm not tall by any means. Where did she suddenly get the strength to do that? I may have underestimated the senior citizen population. I stretch my sore limbs and brush the debris and dead pine needles from my clothes. "Thank you. I'm really sorry for any trouble."

She waves me off. "No bother. It's not every day I get to rescue a girl from a drainpipe."

The words *Wow, you're strong for your age* almost come out of my mouth, but that doesn't sound very polite. Instead, silence descends on the woods. I never realized how loud silence could be. A movement by my foot startles me, and I jump to the side. A chipmunk scampers through the leaves and out of sight. I'm suddenly very aware that no one else is around, and glance nervously toward the building. "I should go before, you know, anyone worries about me."

She nods curtly, and points to a large metal piece of equipment a few yards away. "I came out here to turn on the hourly drainage system. Lucky I saw you before I did that or you'd be covered in sludge right now." She turns to go but I reach out for her arm. When she stops, I'm surprised, since I hadn't planned on reaching out at all.

"Yes?" she asks.

"Uh, nothing," I reply. But I don't let go. What if I left something off my list? Before I can stop myself, I blurt out, "What did you mean before about my not getting what I want? Or what I need? Or something?"

She gently, but firmly, pulls her arm away and gestures toward the main building. "Right now what you need is to rejoin your group before they leave you here."

I follow her gaze and see the group filing out of the building and heading toward the bus. When I turn back, she's gone! I run over to the big metal thing, and then duck around it. The only thing I find is a startled squirrel who takes off up a tree.

A moment later I run onto the bus, out of breath, my brain swirling. The doors whoosh closed behind me. I plop down in my usual seat next to Annabelle. She turns toward me with her open and cheerful face and says, "If I have to watch that boring video one more time, I will fall to my knees and beg for mercy."

I know I shouldn't be surprised, but I'd have thought she'd at least question why I have mud caked on various clothes and body parts. Maybe when I'm twelve, people will finally take more notice of me. I push the old woman's cryptic words out of my head, exhale, and say, "Me too."

Chapter Two

In four hours and fifty-three minutes, the clock on my bright yellow wall will strike midnight. Jupiter will align with Mars. And I will finally be twelve years old. I bet my parents are hoping I'll forget some of the things they've promised me over the years. But I've been writing them all down so not a single one slips through the cracks. I plan to present them with the list very soon.

I think Annabelle is as excited about my birthday as I am. I'm sure it hasn't been easy for her to have a best friend whose parents are so overprotective. Annabelle's been doing most of the things on my list for years now, like buying her own lunch in the cafeteria and walking to school and owning her own cell phone (since she was eight!). She had her ears pierced when she was just three months old. THREE

MONTHS! She has five older brothers, so by the time Annabelle came along her parents were very broken in. My parents, on the other hand, met in college and got married the day after graduation. I came along a year later. They claim that as "young" parents, they remember their teen years all too well. Somehow this translates into trying to keep me totally sheltered. Now that they're thirty-four, they don't seem very young to me. But they're still younger than Annabelle's parents, who are nearly *fifty*. To Annabelle's parents, the teen years are one big blur. She's so lucky!

In preparation for the Big Day, I've decided to get rid of some of my more childish possessions, and surround myself with only age-appropriate objects. There's nothing I can do about my flowered bedspread or the Kermit the Frog shade of green carpet or the yellow walls, but everything else is fair game. I scoop up the macaroni necklace I made when I was five and toss it into the big box on my bed. It lands on top of the old feety pajamas with Dora the Explorer on them and the latest issue of *Highlights*, which my grandmother has finally agreed to stop sending me. I raid my drawers. Anything with a decal of a rainbow, a picture of a unicorn, or my name embroidered on it gets tossed. I push aside the good memories that come floating back as I grab each shirt. I'll make even better memories in clothes that don't look like a six-year-old would wear them.

A few more arts-and-crafts projects, a lamp in the shape of a snowman, and my shelves are pretty bare. Except for my bookshelf. Packing away my books is going to be really hard. I decide that if I haven't read a book in the last year, into the box it goes. The thing is, I have a tendency to read my favorite books over and over, so the pile in the box is pretty small. I force myself to toss in some of the books that are really too young for me, no matter how often I still read them. Then I bring the snowman lamp back out of the box. It might be childish, but a girl needs to see.

Now on to the walls. The only poster on my wall is of Snoopy lying on top of his doghouse looking up at the stars. It's the first poster that was turned into a puzzle at Dad's factory. I feel a pang of guilt, but seriously, it has to go. No self-respecting twelve-year-old has a picture of Snoopy on her wall. I lift up a bottom corner as carefully as I can. It rips and I wince. By the time I peel it all the way off, it has ripped twice more and is really not worth saving.

I save it anyway. Then I examine the room to see if I've forgotten anything. My best and favorite bear, Throckmorton McGoobershneeb, watches me from his perch on my pillow. My grandfather put him in my crib when I was born, and I've had him ever since. Apparently, I took him with me everywhere as a baby, and it's a wonder he still has all his arms and legs. It's hard to tell he's a bear at all. Annabelle says he looks more like a pig. His eyes seem to be daring me to throw him in that box.

"Sorry, Throck," I whisper. I avert my eyes and place him inside before I can change my mind. If I'm going to leave childhood behind, I need to do it all the way.

I'm about to lift the box off the bed when my door flies open. Sawyer zooms in, one overall strap swinging crazily. My mom is two steps behind. Sawyer grabs my legs and holds on for dear life.

"Sawyer Andrew Swenson!" Mom says sternly, and reaches around for his arm. He grips my legs tighter and looks up at me with those big blue eyes of his.

"Rory, my Elmo potty is trying to swallow me!"

I pry him off me. "Elmo is not trying to swallow you," I promise him. "At this rate, you're going to be the only kid in diapers when you get to kindergarten."

His eyes widen and he backs up against the closet door.

"Don't tell him that," Mom scolds. "You know how sensitive he is."

I want to remind her that I'm sensitive, too. She knows how hard it's been for me not to be able to do things every other kid my age can. I try to keep my spirits up, but sometimes it's hard. Sawyer doesn't know how easy he's got it. At three years old, all it takes to make him happy is for my dad to burp. Just one burp, and the boy is filled with glee for hours. And a fart? Forget about it. He'll laugh till he practically chokes. I've got to admit, though, that I do benefit a little from his weirdness. His laughing will make *me* laugh, even if I've had a really bad day at school. Plus, all he'll eat is pizza so we have pizza pretty much every night for dinner. He gets bonus points for that. Now, with the big T-W-E-L-V-E looming ever closer on my horizon, my spirits have lifted themselves right back up, even without his help. "Sorry, Sawyer," I tell him, ruffling his hair. "I'm sure you'll figure out the whole potty training thing one of these days." He smiles gratefully and edges closer. I wrinkle my nose. "I think he needs a change."

"Be my guest," Mom says. "If you're going to start babysitting soon, you better get used to it."

I shake my head. "No, thanks. I saw enough of that last month looking for the dime."

"Whose fault was it he swallowed the dime in the first place?"

I pretend not to hear her as I fold up the box top. I had this grand plan of paying Sawyer ten cents to innocently approach my parents and inform them that his sister is the only sixth grader on the planet without a cell phone, but the plan collapsed when Sawyer swallowed the dime, was rushed to the doctor's office, and then handed over to me to "wait for the dime to pass." It was a very long forty-eight hours of examining the contents of Sawyer's diapers, made longer by the fact that I was grounded as punishment for endangering Sawyer's digestive system. Once I turn twelve and get to babysit, at least I'll be getting *paid* for changing diapers. I'm sure I'll be a great babysitter. I already know Rule #1: Don't give coins to toddlers unless you enjoy sifting through what used to be pizza when it went in, but no longer looks (or smells!) anything remotely like pizza when it comes back out.

But really, babysitting is a means to an end. In exchange for the privilege of getting a cell phone, I have to pay for my own "replacement insurance." My parents don't trust me not to lose the phone, which, frankly, is a little insulting. I haven't lost anything in at least three weeks, and I didn't really like those socks anyway, so it's not like I cried when I realized I'd left them in the locker room at school.

I've already snooped around the house to find out what model phone they got me. My mother must have changed all her hiding places, though, because I couldn't find it. Hopefully, this means I'll get to pick out my own phone. If so, I know exactly what I want. Hot pink, flip style, qwerty keyboard, touch screen, Internet capable, 12-megapixel camera/video, MP3 player, unlimited pictures and texting. Oh, and you can talk on it, too.

"There's still time to change your mind," my mother says, scooping up the smelly, squirming Sawyer. "You can have a party instead."

Usually I choose having a small party over getting a present (the two options they give me every year), figuring if I have a party, then my friends will get me presents. But it's not like my friends are going to get me a cell phone. (Although one time Annabelle's dad got a free phone through his job and they offered it to me, and my mom was like, "Oh, are they going to pay the bill, too?" And then her dad took it back.)

Mom is watching me hopefully, but I shake my head. "No, thanks, I'm good."

She sighs and slowly closes the door behind her. Poor Mom and Dad. They're not handling this impending birthday very well. It's going to be almost as big a change for them as it will be for me. I suspect they are not going to surrender without a fight. But I'm prepared to counter every argument they throw my way.

After pushing the box to the very back of my closet, it's time to move on to Part Two of my plan for the night. I reach under my bed and feel around for the old red shoe box. I've been putting notes in there for years, and after tomorrow I won't need it anymore. I pat the cover lovingly, then pull off the lid and shake out the contents of the box.

Folded-up notebook paper, old napkins, a brochure, and a place mat from the Willow Falls Diner flutter gently to the floor. The last thing out of the box is a puzzle piece, which lands with a satisfying *plop*. I had been visiting my dad's jigsaw puzzle factory one day over Christmas break last year when I overheard two of my dad's coworkers talking about me. "Cute kid. Too bad she has to wear those dorky glasses. They take up half her face!" (Okay, he might not have said *dorky*, but he may as well have.) The other replied, "Yeah, totally." In response to this conversation, I reached for the bin labeled IRREGULARLY SHAPED AND BROKEN PIECES, found the largest piece, and scribbled "Get contact lenses" on the opposite side.

Now I turn the piece over in my hand before pulling out the giant chart I made for my list. The word FINALLY (short for When I'm Finally Twelve) is written in big fancy letters across the top in my neatest handwriting. I sketched out the design in art class last week when I should have been drawing the inside of an orange. My chart is divided into two halves: BIG THINGS and SMALL THINGS. The Big Things are the ones that require a certain amount of planning (and/or $$) to achieve. I should be able to do the Small Things whenever they come up over the course of a regular day.

It's now time to use my notes to fill in the chart. I can

tell just by the shape of the paper what they say. I pick up the very first one I ever wrote. I was seven. It was dinnertime. We were eating meat loaf (this was pre-Sawyer). I had asked for — and been denied — one yellow-spotted iguana.

"A pet is a huge responsibility," Dad had replied, not even bothering to stop chewing. "You can get one when you're twelve."

"*If* you still want one," Mom had added, clearly hoping I wouldn't.

"When I'm *twelve*?" I'd repeated. "That's a zillion years from now."

"It's only five years," Mom had said. "It'll go by in a flash."

I put down my fork, perhaps a bit forcefully since Dad flashed me one of his rare stern looks. "Five years is forever!" I'd protested. "Five years ago I was *two*!" I've always had excellent addition and subtraction skills.

But they didn't budge. After dinner I had gone directly to my room, ripped a page off my rainbow-colored notepad (receiving a painful paper cut in the process), and wrote, "Get a pet." Then I folded it into a tiny square and looked around for a place to store it for five long years. It had to be somewhere safe, where the ravages of time couldn't hurt it. All I could find was the red shoe box that my new sneakers had come in. It seemed sturdy enough. Plus it was red, my favorite color.

In the five long years that followed, the box slowly filled until the lid barely stayed on. But it did the job, and now I'm ready to get to work sorting out my notes. The most recent one is only a few weeks old, and it's not even a regular note. It's an invitation to Natalie Karp's twelfth birthday party. She's one of the most popular girls in our grade, and I don't even mind that I only got invited because Annabelle and Natalie are, like, second cousins on their moms' side. If Natalie's party had been *before* I turned twelve, I would have had to hear about it afterward from Annabelle and Sari at lunch. Sari's parents are *normal* — which is something no one would ever call my parents — so she can do normal sixth grade stuff. Before, she could only do it with Annabelle. But now the world of boy-girl parties will finally be open to me and I won't get left out anymore. I can't wait!

I lovingly place the invitation to the side, and reach for the others. I have to admit, Mom was right when she said I might change my mind about some things. I no longer have any interest in getting a perm after witnessing the poodle-like results on a girl a year ahead of me at school. I no longer want to be a cheerleader, take juggling classes, or join the *American Idol* Fan Club. After crumpling up and disposing of those four, I'm left with twenty-two items. Twenty-two wonderful promises soon to be fulfilled.

I carefully transcribe my list, and then look over the chart with a certain sense of pride. It is truly a work of art. Much better than the inside of an orange would have been.

1. Get a cell phone.

2. Stay home alone.

3. Get my own screen name so I can IM.

4. Shave my legs.

5. Go to the mall with Annabelle and no Parents.

6. Wear makeup.

7. Get a pet.

8. Babysit.

9. Get my ears pierced.

10. Get contact lenses.

11. Attend Natalie Karp's boy-girl birthday party.

Then on the right side is the list of smaller (but still Very Important and Worthwhile) stuff:

1. Get my own house key.

2. Go to bed at 9:30.

3. Drink coffee.

4. Watch <u>Friday the 13th Part IX</u> (which is a part of family lore because my dad took my mom to see a midnight showing of it on their first date in college, and Mom hid her face on his shoulder during the scary parts and they fell in love right there).

5. Sit in the front seat of the car.

6. Do my homework without anyone checking it.

7. Pick out my own clothes.

8. Use the stove, oven, and electrical appliances without permission or supervision.

9. Walk home from school.

10. Buy lunch in the cafeteria.

11. Ride an upside-down roller coaster (so I don't have to stand on the sidelines like a dork at the Willow Falls annual spring carnival).

I pick up the chart carefully so I don't smudge anything, and my eyes land on the brochure I had put aside when I'd emptied the box. The words on the front cover stare up at me: WELCOME TO THE WILLOW FALLS RESERVOIR TOUR. I take a deep breath and pick it up. Over the last few weeks I'd looked at it many times, still not able to decide what to think. On the back of the brochure I had scribbled the words "You won't get what you want until you see what you need." Maybe the blood flow to my brain had been cut off by the narrow drainpipe and I had simply imagined the old woman and her cryptic words. Even if I hadn't imagined her, she was very old and probably wasn't all "there." Plus, she didn't know all the thought and consideration that had gone into my giant to-do list. I definitely *need* to do all these things.

A knock on the door startles me and the brochure drops to the floor. I hastily flip the chart over and lay it on the bed. I don't want to unveil it until I'm sure the time is right.

Dad ducks his head in. The first thing I see — the first thing anyone sees when Dad appears — is the blue stripe in his otherwise blond hair. It is a constant source of embarrassment. His best friend, Skip, dared him to do it last year for their fifteen-year high school reunion, which is just the sort of thing you'd expect from someone named *Skip*. But then he told Dad he'd pay him fifty dollars for every month he keeps it in. Apparently the money is enough to cover our cable bill. When I begged him to cut off the stripe, he just said, "Sure, and then we'll cut off the cable." So I've learned to love the stripe.

"I just got a strange phone call I thought you'd be interested in," Dad announces. "It was a recorded message from your school."

My heart leaps. Maybe school's cancelled on account of a huge snowstorm heading our way! But no, it's already

April. And tomorrow's Saturday. Plus, we haven't gotten more than a few inches of snow in Willow Falls in eighteen years. Maybe they're calling to wish me a happy birthday? Okay, that one's pretty unlikely, too.

Dad comes in and sits on the edge of my bed. I casually slide the chart off to the side. "So what did the recording say?"

"Well, it appears that the school could use a bit of an overhaul. New science labs, new computers, that sort of thing."

I nod in agreement. "Are they asking for donations from parents or something? Because, honestly, for all the library fines I've had to pay, they should —"

But Dad shakes his head. "It's nothing like that. In fact, I think you might be pretty psyched about this."

Dad always says things like "psyched" and "totally." He thinks it makes him sound hip. He thinks the word *hip* is hip. I don't have the heart to tell him it's not. He pauses and looks around the room. "Where's all your stuff? Your shelves are totally bare."

"In a box in my closet. So what will I be psyched about?"

"Why is all your stuff in a box? Are you moving out?" He winks as he says that last part.

"*Daaaad.* Just tell me what the school said."

"*Rooory,*" he says, imitating my whine perfectly. "Just tell me why the only thing on your shelves is dust."

I sigh. My dad doesn't give up easily. "In a few hours I'm going to be twelve. That's, like, almost a teenager. I didn't want all that kid stuff hanging around anymore."

He looks thoughtful, and then says, "When I was a child, I spake as a child, I understood as a child, I thought as a child: But when I became a man, I put away childish things."

"Come again?"

He smiles. "It's a quote from the Bible. I heard it once and it's always stuck with me."

The Bible? If my dad quotes something, it's usually from *The Simpsons* or an old comic book in his collection. "'Spake'?" I repeat. "Is that even a word?" I glance anxiously at the clock. I only have a few hours left to go and so much more to do. "Um, Dad, can you just tell me about the phone call?"

He twists around on the bed. "Where's Throckmorton?"

"Dad!"

He grins. "All right, all right, I'll get down to it. So apparently your principal had an offer that will bring in enough money to totally modernize the school. For the next six weeks, they're going to be filming a movie there."

My eyes widen. A *movie*? Here in Willow Falls? Nothing exciting like that has *ever* happened in our sleepy little town.

"They called everyone to assure us the filming won't disrupt the learning process," he continues. "I don't know if I —"

I cut him off. "Who's in it?"

He pauses to think. "Um, the star is some boy named Jake. Jake Henderson? Hamilton?"

My breath catches in my throat. "Jake *Harrison*?"

"Yes, that's it. Harrison."

"Is this a joke? They really called about some school board election or something, and you're just trying to kill me?"

He laughs. "Nope. I'm not that clever. Who's Jake Harrison?"

"Only the coolest, hottest fourteen-year-old boy in this or any other universe!"

"How can someone be hot and cool at the same time? Don't they cancel each other out?"

"Not when they're Jake Harrison!" I start clapping my hands in excitement, like I'm Sawyer's age and watching my first fireworks.

"Since when did you start liking boys anyway?" Dad asks, in a tone both breezy and dead serious.

I stop clapping and instantly redden. If he'd asked me this question a few months ago, I'd have made a face and said that I'd rather eat a centipede than kiss a boy. And I HATE centipedes. It really used to bother me when Annabelle and Sari would go on and on about the cuteness of various sixth grade boys. It was just one more thing they had in common that I didn't. But over the last few months, I'd started to see what they meant and could finally join in the conversation. And now? If it meant I got to kiss Jake Harrison? I'd eat that centipede in a heartbeat. At least, I'm pretty sure I would.

But talk to my dad about boys? That I know I can't do. I mumble words like "growing up" and "the facts of life" and bolt for the door.

"Where are you going?" he calls after me.

From halfway down the stairs I yell, "I've got to call Annabelle!"

"Don't bother," Mom says, as I hit the bottom step. She holds the phone out to me. "I'm expecting an important call, so if it comes through, I'll need you to get off."

I nod and snatch the phone.

"Rory?" the voice on the other end is screaming. "Rory? Is that you? Can you believe it?"

"No!" I yell back. "My dad just told me! You think it's for real?" I follow my mom back to the kitchen and pace in circles around the table.

"It's totally for real!" Annabelle says. "We've all been texting about it. Natalie says they're going to be hiring extras to be in the movie. Like us kids, but we'd have to pretend to be real schoolkids, and since we ARE real schoolkids we'll definitely get the job!"

Normally I'd bristle at the fact that, once again, I was left out of the loop. Everyone was texting except for me. But now, with my own phone nearly within my grasp and with Jake Harrison to think about, I let it go. "How can we get picked for it? Do we audition and then —" But my words are interrupted by the call-waiting beep. Mom notices my pause and looks up from the table where she's been clipping coupons. I don't think my mom's ever bought anything in her life without a coupon or one of those store discount cards. She is very thrifty.

"Is that my call?" she asks.

I grit my teeth and tell Annabelle I have to hang up.

"That's okay. I'll talk to you tomorrow. Sari keeps texting me and I can't write back while I'm on the phone."

We say good-bye and I hand the phone over to Mom. One more day. Just one more day till Annabelle won't need to call me on my parents' phone. Soon I won't feel like I'm competing for Annabelle's attention all the time because I'll be able to text, too. I nearly skip back upstairs to my room. I'm relieved to see that Dad is no longer staring sadly at my empty shelves. I close the door behind me and move the chart over to my desk. I have one last goal to add on the Big Things side.

12. Meet Jake Harrison.

I'm so delirious with anticipation of the near future that it takes me a few minutes to notice the pamphlet from the class trip on my pillow. That's strange. I don't remember picking it up from the floor. Dad must have found it and put it there. But instead of the drawing of a water tunnel leading into a glistening reservoir that I expect to see, a photograph of a cell phone adorns the cover. "Yay!!" I scream, grabbing it. "It's finally happening!" I do a little dance around my room, then calm down enough to look at the pamphlet more closely. Is that . . . why is there . . . huh? The photograph shows what looks like a normal phone, but there are only two buttons on it. Just two. How is that possible? I flip open the brochure. WELCOME TO YOUR CHILD'S FIRST PHONE. THE ONLY TWO NUMBERS HE OR SHE WILL EVER NEED!

My hands start to shake as I read on. GIVE YOUR CHILD

THE SECURITY OF KNOWING HE OR SHE CAN ALWAYS REACH YOU OR EMERGENCY SERVICES. SIMPLY PROGRAM YOUR HOME OR OFFICE PHONE NUMBER INTO BUTTON NUMBER 1 AND 911 INTO THE OTHER.

I sink down onto the bed as I read the last line. BUT WAIT, THERE'S MORE! OUR BUILT-IN GPS TRACKER WILL ALWAYS ALERT YOU IF YOUR CHILD LEAVES THE DESIGNATED AREA. YOU'LL KNOW WHERE HE OR SHE IS AT EVERY MOMENT. NOW *THAT'S* PEACE OF MIND WORTH PAYING FOR!

I stare at the words. Two buttons. No texting. No megapixels. No MP3. Just Mom and the police. Oh, and a GPS tracking my every move.

My parents must really, REALLY hate me!

Chapter Three

I find Mom in Sawyer's room, tucking him into bed. I hold up the cell phone pamphlet. "Very funny. You really had me going there for a minute."

"Shh," Mom whispers. "He's almost asleep."

I look down at Sawyer, who is running a plastic yellow race car up the side of his face and making *vroom vroom* noises. "No, he's not."

"Well, he's never going to fall asleep with you yakking."

I take a deep breath and exhale. "Mom, can we please talk about this?"

"About what?" she asks, purposely not meeting my eyes.

I groan and go off in search of Dad, who will hopefully be more forthcoming. I find him at the dining room table, bent over a huge poster of a mountain range. He draws a quick zigzag shape on it, then stands back to look. Even though he has a full-time puzzle designer on staff, he likes to come up with his own patterns, too, and can often be found working on them late into the night. He never brings his tools home, though. Not after that unfortunate incident in third grade. I instinctively run my hand over the scar on my elbow.

I wait until he erases his line — as he always does — before interrupting. As soon as he's blown away the last bit of eraser dust, but before he can draw another pattern, I lay the brochure down in front of him. "Is this for real, Dad?"

He picks it up with a grin. "Isn't it great? Don't you love it?"

There are so many ways to respond to that question. I pause and choose my words carefully. "It only has two buttons."

"And a built-in GPS tracker!" he says as proudly as if he'd built the phone himself.

"Dad, I'm begging you. I need a phone with more than two buttons."

He tilts his head at me. "Are you sure?"

I nod vehemently.

He sighs. "Your mom thought you might feel that way."

He leaves the room and returns a minute later with a big cardboard box.

Relief floods through me. "You got me a real phone after all!"

"Not exactly," he says.

I squint up at him suspiciously. "What do you mean?"

He pushes the box into my arms. "We picked up brochures for twenty different phones and service plans. Your job, if you choose to accept it, is to go over the material, choose the one you think makes the most sense for your needs and is the most economical for the family, and then explain to us why. If we agree with your assessment, you can get the phone."

Stricken, I look down at the contents of the box. Sure enough, it's full of exactly what he said.

"A chart with graphics might be nice," he adds, turning back to his puzzle.

I don't move. How can this end well? Even if I manage to sort through everything and make sense of it, how am I going to convince them to let me get the one I want?

He glances up. "You're still here? I thought you'd be halfway through the box by now."

I shift my weight so the box doesn't slip. "How am I supposed to figure this out? Service plans and all that?"

"You're good with math," he says. "You'll do fine."

When I don't answer, he adds, "Or you can just take the one with the two buttons."

"And built-in GPS tracker," I mutter, hurrying from the room.

"Have fun!" he calls after me.

As I pass Sawyer's room, Mom glances up from her perch on the side of his bed. She sees the box and smiles. I smile back, as breezily as I can muster. I can't let them see me sweat.

By the time I finish comparing and contrasting the pros and cons of each of the twenty phones and various calling/texting/photo/video/Internet/GPS options, it is almost midnight. The only time I'm allowed to stay up this late is on New Year's Eve, and even then I'm usually asleep on the couch well before the clock strikes twelve. Mom and Dad have come in five times to try to get me to finish this tomorrow, but even though I'm delirious with exhaustion, I'm not going to quit. I've narrowed it down to the three they're most likely to agree to, even though they are SO far away from my original vision.

My legs creak from sitting so long and my head feels like it's under water. How am I going to stay awake to practice my presentation? For a second I debate making a cup of coffee (#3 on the Small Things list) to help keep me awake, but figure since it also requires #8, Use the Stove, Oven, and Electrical Appliances Without Permission or Supervision, I decide to just wash my face with cold water instead. But somehow, before I can make it into the bathroom, I wind up sprawled across my bed. The last thing I remember is trying to decide if rollover minutes are a better deal than unlimited calling to in-network customers.

• • • • • • • • • • •

I wake up with a spring in my step and a smile on my face. I'm twelve! *Look out, world, here comes Rory Swenson!* I leap off the bed, slide halfway across the floor on top of the phone brochures, and slam into the door. Shaking it off, I tear downstairs at top speed. Usually on my birthday a big plate of chocolate chip pancakes is waiting for me, the kitchen table aglow with birthday candles for me to wish on. But when I reach the kitchen this morning, the only things waiting for me on the table are a note and a bowl of Corn Flakes. My spirits sink. Couldn't Mom at least have made it a bowl of Cap'n Crunch? According to the note, Mom took Sawyer to his Yoga for Toddlers class, Dad is out mowing the lawn, and I shouldn't forget to put the milk away when I'm finished with it. I have to squint to see HAPPY BIRTHDAY scrawled at the bottom.

I'm about to resign myself to eating the cereal, alone, when it dawns on me that I can have anything I want. I can fry an egg. I can flip pancakes. I can boil oatmeal. Sure, I don't actually know how to *do* any of those things, but how hard could it be? I turn my back on the cold cereal and hurry over to the pantry. My stomach growls in anticipation. I pull out the bag of chocolate chips and the pancake mix. I read the side of the box. *To make 6–7 pancakes: Mix 2½ cups pancake mixture, 2 eggs, 3¼ cups water, ½ cup oil; stir until smooth; pour into greased frying pan at medium heat.*

WAY too hard. I'll just eat the chocolate chips instead. As I close the pantry, the back door swings open and the smell of freshly mown grass wafts my way. It almost, but not quite, covers the smell coming off Dad.

"Is something burning?" Dad asks, hurrying over to the stove. He puts his hand a few inches above it to feel for heat.

I put my hands on my hips. "Very funny. Why would you think I'd try to cook something?"

"Because I know you," he says, chuckling. Then he glances at the sink, checking for dirty pans and bowls, no doubt. "Patience isn't your strong suit. I bet you have a whole list of all the things you can do now that you're twelve. Including using the stove by yourself."

I open my mouth to argue, but really, what's the point? "Okay, I have a list, but how can you say I don't have patience? I've waited patiently for twelve years! I could have sneaked around and done half the stuff on my list already, but I didn't. If that's not patience, I don't know what is."

He brightens. "You're absolutely right. I should trust you to make the right choices now." He reaches out to hug me.

I step back, holding my nose. "Shower first, please."

He laughs and flips a switch on the fancy-schmancy coffee/cappuccino/espresso maker that Mom won in a raffle last year. It gurgles to life as he heads out of the kitchen. I guess I have no choice but to have cereal for breakfast.

Or *do* I?

I remove my hand from my nose and inhale the aroma of the brewing coffee. Or cappuccino or espresso. I have no idea what the difference is. Whatever it's called, it smells good. It smells very good. Hurrying across the room, I grab a mug from the counter along the way. I've seen my parents put their cups under the spigot a thousand times, but when I put mine there, nothing happens. I look all around the machine. Rows of buttons and levers and knobs stare back. Why would someone make a coffee machine so complicated? What was so wrong with the old one with the big coffeepot under it? I push and twist anything that looks pushable or twistable. A hiss here, a sputter there, but nothing pours out into the cup. I pull the mug back out, then stick it in again. This time I hear a faint *click*. Within seconds, a nice thin stream of black coffee/cappuccino/espresso or whatever it is flows into my mug, steam rising gently into the air. Soon the mug is nearly full. How do I get it to stop? I pull and push and twist again, but it just keeps coming out. I'm beginning to panic. All other options failing, I yank the cup out. I'm so busy hopping up and down due to the hot coffee that has spilled out of the over-flowing mug and onto my bare feet that I don't immediately notice the stream of coffee now pouring out of the machine and onto the counter. By the time I recover, the coffee has made its way over the edge of the counter and is heading down the white cabinets.

I told my mom that white was a risky choice for a kitchen, but did she listen? She did not.

My first thought is to cup my hands beneath the flow, but luckily common sense prevails. Instead I shove another mug under the spigot, and thankfully the coffee dribbles to a stop just before reaching the top. It takes half a roll of paper towels to sop up the mess.

When I'm sure not a drop remains on any surface, I turn back to my mug. It still feels hot, so I drop in an ice cube. While I'm waiting for it to dissolve, I skim a "Dear

Abby" letter about whether it's necessary to send a thank-you note to thank someone for sending *you* a thank-you note. It isn't.

When I pick it up again, my mug feels much less likely to leave a third-degree burn on my palm. I inhale deeply, take my first sip, and promptly spit it back into the mug.

THIS is what all the fuss is about? THIS is what makes people wait in line at coffee shops for hours? Then I remember I'm supposed to add things to it. I pour some of the coffee into the sink to make room for the milk, which I pour in till it reaches the top. Then I add a few Sweet'N Lows from the counter. Ah, much better. I almost can't taste the original coffee at all.

I keep drinking. I hear Dad upstairs on the phone. While I wait for him to join me so he can see how grown up I look with my coffee, I drink some more. Before I know it, I've finished it and gone on to the second mug. By the time Dad comes in, I've finished it off.

He looks from me, to the empty cup in my hand, to the empty cup on the counter, to the also-empty coffee machine, and raises his brows.

I hold up the cup to show him, and grin broadly. "I drink coffee now!"

"Um, Rory? Is your arm shaking, or are we having an earthquake?"

"What do you mean?"

He tilts his head at my arm. I follow his gaze. It is, in fact, shaking! A lot, actually. That's weird. Why is my arm shaking?

Dad lifts the bag to pour more coffee into the machine. He is moving oddly. First in these fast bursts, then really slow. "Why are you moving like that?" I shout.

"Like what?" he asks. "And why are you shouting at me?"

"I'm not shouting," I shout. Maybe I am. My head feels funny.

As the machine starts to gurgle again, he asks, "Exactly how much coffee did you drink?"

"Not a lot, I mean . . ." I pause here because it sounds like I can hear an echo of my own voice from far away. This makes my thoughts turn to the beach over the summer, when Sawyer pressed a conch shell to my ear and I could hear the ocean and it was very cool. Although now that I think about it, we had been standing right *next* to the ocean, so that might explain it.

For some reason, Dad is waving his hand in front of my face. His hand looks strange. Like he has too many fingers. "Yes, Dad?"

"Would two of these big mugfuls be a good guess?"

I look down at the mug still in my shaking hand. "Is that a lot?" I ask.

"That's like six regular cups!" he says, his brows creasing in concern. He takes the mug from me and places it in the sink. "For someone who's never drank coffee before, well, I think you better go lie down a while."

"I'm fine. Seriously."

"Then why are you bouncing up and down on your toes like you're about to lift off into space?"

I didn't realize I was bouncing. "Um, because I'm excited it's my birthday?"

He doesn't buy it and marches me to my room. He points to the bed, then leaves and shuts the door. I hop nimbly around the strewn brochures, then dutifully lie down, not feeling at all tired. What was *in* that coffee? Oh, right. *Caffeine.* I sit up, my attention drawn to my fingers and toes, which seem to be moving to the beat of some song I can't hear. Gotta get up and do something. I'd clean my room, but packing most of it up last night has left me without anything to clean. I look down at my coffee-splattered pajamas and sprint over to my dresser. I yank out one item of clothing after the next. What's the perfect outfit for a twelfth birthday? This shirt's too big. That one's too small. Too bright. Too dark. I finally pick out a top and a bottom and throw them on. I glance at the clock and am surprised to see that only four minutes have passed. Weird. I might as well work on my phone presentation. I sit down at my desk, and the next thing I know, my mother is shaking me awake. Whoa. I fell asleep? How did I fall asleep when I was so totally wide awake? I sit up and my chart slips onto the floor. So much for working on my presentation. But as I bend to pick it up, I see that the entire thing is filled in! The memory of filling it in filters back slowly and choppily, like remembering a dream. Note to Self: No More Coffee for a Long, Long Time. If ever. I quickly lean over to cover the chart. No use giving Mom a sneak peak.

She raises an eyebrow, but only says, "Ten minutes. Family room."

"I'll be there," I promise as I glance casually at my hand to test for shaking. Seems pretty steady. Wouldn't want to be a surgeon about to operate on a patient, but since that's really not a concern, I think I'm in the clear.

"Oh, and Rory?" she says, halfway out the door. "That's quite a . . . *colorful* outfit."

She closes the door behind her. I look down and shudder. Black-and-white-striped shorts and a pink polka-dot shirt. The fashion police would definitely give me a ticket for "Dressing While Over-Caffeinated."

I spend the next nine minutes preparing for the presentation. First I change into clothes that don't make me look like a character on Cartoon Network (and which should have been packed away in my box yesterday), and then brush my teeth twice to get rid of the icky combination of coffee and sleep breath. Finally, I pull my hair into a low ponytail (which Mom always says makes me look more mature) and resign myself to my fate.

When I arrive in the family room, I find Mom on the couch and Dad in his easy chair, both with arms crossed. Usually the wood paneling and thick brown carpet in this room relax me, but right now nothing's going to slow down my racing heart. An easel has been set up across from them, and I hoist the poster onto it. I'm careful not to reveal my FINALLY chart on the opposite side, since I wouldn't want to scare them off at this crucial moment. Plenty of time for that. I run the plan through my head again. Don't whine or beg. No sulking. Keep eye contact at all times. Stand tall. Sound responsible and confident. Remember that even though these finalists are the most restrictive, boring, lame cell phones in the history of cell phones, they are better than the one with two buttons.

I take a deep breath and begin. "What you see here are my top three choices. All of them have prepaid plans so I can't run up a huge bill. All will allow you, the parents, to control the usage of my phone. You can set the limit for talking and texting, and on this one" — I point to the last of the three — "you can even control which phone numbers I can accept calls from."

"Really? Huh." My father nods appreciatively. "I like that last option."

I smile broadly, encouragingly. Maybe I worried for nothing. This might not be so bad. Then Mom turns to Dad and says, "But do you really think she needs one at all? Isn't it just asking for trouble?"

My smile fades. "But Mom," I begin, then cut myself off. *Do not whine.* I start again, lighter and breezier. "I understand your fears, Mom. But you don't have to worry. I won't talk to strangers, I won't text Annabelle during dinner, and I won't take embarrassing pictures and post them on the Internet."

"That's all well and good," she says, "but generations of kids survived just fine without cell phones. Why wouldn't you?"

For this one, I have an answer all prepared. "Yes, but those generations didn't have to worry about gangs and drugs and all the violence inspired by video games and television shows."

Dad laughs. "Gangs? In Willow Falls?"

I redden. "Okay, maybe not gangs. But the other stuff."

In a shaky voice my mother asks, "Are there drugs at your school? Because if that's the case, maybe we need to move or —"

"No, Mom," I say hurriedly. "Don't worry. Forget the gangs and drugs. I didn't mean it." She sags back onto the couch.

I have to scramble to get back on track. In my most calm and professional voice, I say, "But studies have proven that having a cell phone is an excellent idea. What if I'm stranded somewhere or the school bus breaks down or —"

Dad holds up his hand. "Okay, honey, you've made your point. As long as you agree to use part of your allowance to insure the phone against its inevitable loss, then you can have that third one on the list. I'll take you this afternoon."

My heart soars. I'm not even insulted at Dad's implying I will lose the phone. I'll just have to prove I can hold on to it.

"Just a minute," Mom says, and just as quickly, my heart sinks. "What about the GPS tracking feature of that one we offered you last night? If you're going to be more independent, I want to know where you are."

I sigh. I knew she wouldn't give up on the two-button phone so easily. "This phone has a GPS on it," I tell her, trying to keep my voice light. "All of them do now. So if I go missing, the police will be able to find me. Plus, the whole idea is that with a phone, you'll be able to call me anytime you want, so you'll always know where I am."

Dad turns to Mom. "Come on, Robin, you're scaring yourself. Rory can handle her own cell phone without us having to track her every move. We've got to trust her to make the right choices now that she's twelve."

He winks at me. I smile back gratefully.

"Fine," Mom says, standing up. "You can get the third one on your chart. Well done on the chart, by the way."

"Thanks," I reply, pleased.

"But the first time I call and you don't answer, you're giving back the phone."

I'm about to point out how unreasonable that is, when Dad says, "Robin, that's a bit unreasonable." I love my dad. Mom opens her mouth to argue, but Sawyer chooses this moment to run in and announce that his copy of *Is Your Mama a Llama?* has "fallen" into the toilet. Gotta hand it to that kid. He has a great sense of timing. I might even let him look at my new phone.

From, like, a hundred feet away.

Before Dad and I leave, I flip the chart over so the FINALLY side is on full display for whoever might happen to stroll by and read it. After all, Mom did say I'm good at charts, and this is the best one yet.

Chapter Four

"Why are you driving so fast?" I shout. My hands grip the sides of the seat for dear life as we careen down the street. "Dad, you're right on top of that car!" I let go of the seat and my hands fly up over my face. I never thought I'd die on my birthday. Just when I'm finally going to get everything I ever wanted, I'll never get the chance. It doesn't seem fair.

Dad laughs. "I'm nowhere near him. Things just look different from the front seat."

When a few more seconds pass without a crash, I allow myself to peek through my fingers. He's right. Things *do* look different up here. Without the back of Mom's or Dad's seat to obstruct my view, I can see *everything*. I feel like I'm sitting right on the hood of the car. I lean forward and tentatively touch the dashboard, and then the front window. Probably thick enough to stop me from flying through it if he stops short. Maybe I'll survive long enough to get my phone, after all. Still, I double (then triple) check that my seat belt is securely fastened.

After we learn that the store down on Main Street doesn't sell our model, I try to convince Dad to go for one of the other two on my chart, both of which are in stock.

"Have you *met* your mother?" he asks, heading toward the door. "We can't come home with anything other than the one we agreed on."

I sigh. "You're right. Let's keep looking."

At the next store, a young clerk wearing a tie covered with Snoopy in various poses greets us eagerly at the door. I want to ask him where he got the tie so I can get it for Dad for Christmas, but there's a time and a place for everything and right now time is of the essence. We have to meet Mom and Sawyer across town for my birthday dinner in a little over an hour. If I don't find the phone before then, I'll have to wait till next weekend. And that's WAY too long to wait.

The clerk backs away in make-believe horror when my dad tells him the name and model of the phone we're looking for. "You don't want that one," he booms. "There are much cooler phones out there, for sure."

I can feel my cheeks beginning to burn.

"I'm sure there are," Dad says firmly, "but we need this one."

The guy lets out a long whistle and shakes his head. "No can do, I'm afraid. We haven't got any. Well, just the open-box one, but you wouldn't want that one."

"What does 'open-box' mean?" I ask.

The clerk glances around as though looking for where the sound of my voice came from. He seems surprised when he sees me in front of him. I'm used to this.

He recovers and explains, "An open-box item is used for display. We can sell it if it's the last one in stock."

I jump up. "I'll take it!"

"You sure?" he asks. "Those things get pretty banged up. Kids playing with them all day." He shudders. "I sure wouldn't want it."

"Let's just take a look at it," Dad says wearily.

"You're the boss, man," he says, returning a minute later with the phone. It looks just like the one in the brochure. Not the prettiest of phones, and texting will be a royal pain since there's no qwerty keyboard, but once I have it, no one will leave me out of important conversations anymore, and that's the most important thing.

"We'll take it!" I repeat.

"I think you should try it first, honey," Dad says. "Call me on my phone; see how it works."

He whips out his own cell phone, which he claims to use only for business. But I've seen him checking football scores when he's not home to watch the games.

I start dialing Dad's number. When I hit the three button, the three doesn't appear on the little screen. I press harder. Nothing. I hold it up to the guy. "Um, the three doesn't seem to work."

"Guess you could always find friends without a three in their number," the guy jokes, holding out his hand.

For a second my grip tightens on the phone. Maybe I could convince everyone I know with a three to change their number to one without one. Dad nudges my arm and I have to concede that it's not the best plan. "Fine." I drop the phone into the guy's palm. "Thanks anyway."

"Sorry," he says. "Hey, if you were gonna take that one, maybe you'd be interested in this." He heads off to the desk and grabs something from a bottom drawer. When he returns, what does he hold up? The phone with the two buttons!

"What do you think?" the guy asks, grinning. "This way you'd never have to worry about the three breaking. Get it? Because there aren't any numbers!"

Before Dad can decide that maybe this phone isn't such a bad idea after all, I grab his arm. "Let's go, Dad."

"Guess we should have called around first," he says as

we step out onto the sidewalk. Then he chuckles. "Ah, the irony of having to *call* to find a phone."

I'm pretty sure he's trying to make a joke. He gets a smile in response because I'm trying very hard to remain calm and be a team player. It's getting harder by the minute.

Only one other place in town sells cell phones, and Dad drives at breakneck speed to the mall. Admittedly it probably just *seems* like breakneck speed because of the whole front seat thing throwing off my perspective on everything. Or maybe the caffeine crazies are making a comeback. Either way, it feels like we make it to the mall in record time. Usually my dad drags out the drive to the mall because he hates it so much. He claims to have *mall-o-phobia* — a fear of malls and all the materialism they hold within. Between him and my mom, it's really a miracle I have any clothes or shoes at all.

Once we're inside, I practically have to run to keep up with Dad's long strides. We quickly pass the pet store where I'll be getting my pet one day soon, the earrings store where I'll be getting my ears pierced, and all the other stores I can finally go into now without Dad tapping his foot impatiently or Mom steering me away because she doesn't have a coupon for it.

Dad scurries along, eyes down, with his hands held up to the right side of his face like he's shielding it from the sun. "Dad, seriously," I plead. "People are going to think you stole something."

"I'll take my chances," he says without looking up.

"You know, just because you see something in a store window doesn't mean you have to buy it."

"These places are tricky," he warns. "They lure you in with their shiny wares and lifetime guarantees. The only way to win is not to look." To prove it, he closes his eyes and flings himself past the CD store and the hot-pretzel stand in a single bound. It's a good thing no one from school is here to see this.

When we reach the phone store, he straightens up and adjusts his jacket and looks as normal as possible for a guy in his thirties with a blue stripe in his hair. Twenty-three minutes later, the saleswoman hands me my phone. Truly. My own phone. With a working *three*. And the other nine numbers, too! And a free pink case thanks to a coupon Mom slipped me earlier! As we walk back through the mall, I keep putting it in different pockets to see which is the most comfortable. Then I try the pockets in my backpack, which I carry everywhere.

Dad stops suddenly as we near the exit. This is surprising. Usually he sprints the last twenty yards to the door. "Are you going to be all right if I duck into the men's room?"

"Hey, if anything happens to me, I'll just call for help!"

"Just stay right there," he says, pointing to a bench. He hands me the bag from the phone store, before looking around to make sure no one's lurking nearby to grab me.

I had promised Annabelle she'd be my first call. I reach into my back pocket for the phone. Then the other back pocket. Then my front pockets. I empty my backpack onto the bench. A dollar bill, a copy of *The Secret Garden*, two ponytail holders, and half a stick of Juicy Fruit tumble out. But no phone. I look through the bag from the store: empty box, phone charger, manual, receipt. I take everything out one at a time. Then I start to panic. I flip my hair over and shake it out as though the phone would actually fall from it. I yank at the bottom of my shirt. Nothing. I drop to my knees and search under the bench.

"Whatcha doing?" Dad asks, his head suddenly appearing next to mine. I hurry to stand up.

"Um, you didn't happen to, ah . . . um . . ." I stop, unable to form the words.

"Did I what?" he asks, eyes already focused on the exit doors.

I take a deep breath. Might as well get this over with. "I can't find my phone."

I have his full attention now. His eyes widen, and then he bursts out laughing. Big guffaws. So big that shoppers are turning to stare. Wiping tears from his eyes, he says, "You're kidding, right?"

I shake my head miserably. This sends him into another fit of hysterics. Now a small crowd has formed.

"I've got to sit down," he says, sitting on the bench. His shoulders continue to shake with silent laughter. Still annoying, but at least it's quieter.

"Is your father all right?" a woman loaded down with shopping bags asks. "Do you want to use my cell phone to call for help?"

"No, no," my dad chokes out. "My daughter has her own phone. No, wait, she doesn't!" This sends him off into another gale of laughter.

I puff out my cheeks grimly and turn to the woman. "Thanks anyway."

She gives us a strange look, but moves along, bags swinging. Another woman and her young son linger to see what's going to happen. Seeing them reminds me that we have to meet Mom and Sawyer soon. But I can't leave the mall without my phone, I just can't.

"Okay, Dad, you've had your fun. Now can we please go look for my phone? It has to be here somewhere."

He gives one more guffaw, then wipes his eyes again and stands up. "C'mon." He puts his hand on my shoulder. "Let's go retrace our steps."

We walk back exactly the way we came, scanning the ground, nearby benches, and inside fake potted plants. Just a lot of dust and a stray dime. We even duck into the stores along the way to ask if anyone turned it in. Dad suggests we try calling it, but I can't remember the number they assigned me. Finally we end up back at the phone store again.

"Hi again," says the nice woman who had sold us the phone. "Did you forget something?"

Dad pushes me forward. Unable to meet her eyes, I whisper, "Um, I seem to have lost my phone."

She leans over the counter a bit. "I'm sorry, what did you say, hon?"

"I lost my phone," I say louder, cringing with every word.

Her face lights up. "Hey, Robby!" she calls out over her shoulder. "We've got a winner!"

Robby must be the manager because he hurries out of the back room with a notebook in his hand. "Seriously?" He flips the book open. "Someone beat four hours?"

The woman nods happily and gestures to me with her thumb. "Fifteen minutes!"

Robby nods appreciatively. "Well done, young lady!" He jots something down in the notebook and then flips it closed.

"I'm, um, glad I could make everyone so happy." I glance

at my dad. I can tell by the way his face is contorted that he's trying to stifle another outburst. "But can I have another phone now?"

Robby turns to the woman. "Did they buy the replacement insurance?"

She nods. "The works."

I'm sure it's taking all of Dad's self-control not to say, *I told you you'd be glad you used all your allowance from the last six months to buy the insurance policy.*

"All right, just give us a few minutes to deactivate the old phone and activate your new one." Robby reaches for the bag, which I realize I'm clutching with both hands. I release it, and he pulls out the paperwork and heads over to a computer at the end of the long desk. The woman turns to the next customer, her eyes still crinkling.

"Dad," I ask while we wait, "do you think you could not tell Mom about this? If she knew I lost it already, she'll say this proves I'm not responsible enough to have it in the first place."

"She doesn't really think that," he assures me. "She's just having a hard time with you growing up, that's all. She'll come around."

I notice he didn't agree not to tell her, but I have a feeling he won't. I hope he's right that she'll come around, because I'll need her help for a lot of the things on my list.

Even though she can drive me crazy, I still kinda miss the time we used to spend together pre-Sawyer.

Store employees keep nudging one another and looking over at us. Dad takes pity on me and suggests I wait across the hall in the pet store. I run out before he's even finished the sentence.

The pet store smells a bit ripe. The only other person in here is a teenage boy in a blue sweatshirt buying dog food. I try to breathe only through my mouth as I pass the cages of assorted hamsters and guinea pigs. I forget the smell, though, as soon as I see the bunny. White fluffy body, orange floppy ears, warm and caring eyes. The bunny of my dreams. My heart beats faster. His little nose twitches happily when I stick my hand up to the wire cage. I immediately recognize him as the sweetest, softest, most loving bunny in the entire world. I hurry around the cage in search of a sign that will tell me how much he costs, but all I see is an index card with his name:

```
Kyle R.
Male rabbit
Eight months old
```

I. MUST. HAVE. HIM. I must also change his name to something cuter than Kyle. I busy myself by making little clicking noises and stroking his nose through the bars. He seems to like it because he keeps lifting his paw at me like he's waving. He is clearly meant to be mine. But what if someone takes him before I can convince my parents of this? I rush to the front counter and wait as patiently as I can (which is to say, not patiently at all) for the boy to finish paying for his dog food. It eventually dawns on me that he doesn't have enough money.

"Why don't you get the cheaper brand?" the store manager suggests.

The boy shakes his head. His hair is so dark it's almost purple. "My grandmother told me to get this one."

"I'm sorry, kid, but you're a dollar short."

The boy turns sideways and I catch a glimpse of his face. His expression is sad and frustrated at the same time. Even though he looks only a year or two older than me, I don't recognize him from school.

I can see Dad heading over from the phone store. The window to find out about my future bunny before Dad drags me away is getting smaller. I reach into my backpack and feel around until my fingers close on the dollar bill. I'm about to hand it to the boy when a certain tilt of his chin tells me he wouldn't accept it. So I crumple it a little and toss it on the floor near his left foot.

"Hey!" I say loudly, pointing to it. "You must have dropped that."

The kid turns in surprise, then follows where I'm pointing. His face lights up. "Thanks!" He makes a move toward it, hesitates for a second, and then in one swift motion picks it up and plunks it down on the counter. The man takes it and hands him the bag of food.

I glance out the door. Dad is only a few of his enormous strides away.

"Thanks again," the boy says as he hurries past me, hugging the bag like it's the dog itself.

I quickly step forward to take his place. "How much is that bunny?"

"That guy?" the manager asks, glancing over at the cage. "He's on special. Twenty bucks. Comes with the cage."

My eyes open wide. Twenty bucks for the bunny AND the cage? That's perfect!

A hand clamps down on my shoulder. "We have to go, Rory."

"Can you hold him for a few days?" I ask as Dad begins steering me out of the store.

"Don't worry," the guy promises, "he'll be here."

"How can you be sure?"

"Trust me."

He must not be a bunny lover, which I just do not understand at all. Who wouldn't love bunnies? "Bye, Kyle!" I call out. "See you soon!"

As soon as he can tear me away from the pet shop window, Dad hands me my new phone and begins the sprint out of the mall. Not taking any chances this time, I grasp it firmly in my hand. By the time we get in the car, my knuckles have turned white from the pressure. I've just fastened my seat belt when the phone rings, startling me so much that it drops into my lap.

"Who could be calling you already?" Dad asks, backing out of the narrow parking spot.

"I have no idea." I fumble with the phone and press the green button with the little picture of a phone receiver on it. "Hello?"

"Yes, hello," a male voice on the other end says. He sounds rushed. "I'll need three large pizzas, one plain with thin crust, one extra cheese, and one with meatballs and onions."

When I'm too surprised to answer, his voice rises. "Did you get all that?"

"Um," I stammer, meeting Dad's questioning glance. "You have the wrong number."

"This isn't Johnny's Pizzeria?" the guy asks, sounding very annoyed now. He must really want his pizza.

"Nope, sorry."

He mutters something R-rated and hangs up.

"I'm sure that was just a fluke," Dad assures me. "A random wrong number."

I'm sure he's right. Kind of funny, really. I dial Annabelle's number. She picks up on the first ring.

"It's me!" I squeal into the phone. "I finally got it!"

"Hurray!" she yells with just the right amount of enthusiasm. "Am I your first call?"

"Yes! But someone already called *me*. To order a pizza! Can you believe it? My first call was a wrong number!"

"You should have told him his order would be ready in twenty minutes!"

I laugh even though I never could have done that.

"I've gotta run," she says. "I just saved your number on my phone. I'm still coming over to watch the movie tonight, right?"

"Yup. Hey, I found a bunny I want!"

"Cool! Later!"

I watch the screen as the call disconnects. My phone doesn't have photo capabilities, and the screen is a dull gray color. But at that moment I don't care at all. It works! And it's mine! I'm still looking at the phone when it rings again.

"Wow, you're popular," Dad comments.

"I'm sure it's just Annabelle." I press the button. "Hello?"

A high-pitched female voice asks, "I have a coupon for a free liter of Coke with a medium pizza, but it expired last week. Will you still honor it?"

I laugh. "Very funny! But my mother doesn't sound anything like that."

The voice on the other end doesn't laugh. "Excuse me?" she says after a pause.

"Annabelle, I know it's you."

Pause. "Is this Johnny's Pizzeria?" She doesn't sound so much like Annabelle now.

I look down at the screen. The number that shows up isn't Annabelle's! I hurriedly bring it back to my ear. "I'm sorry, you have the wrong number."

"Is this . . ." She rattles off the number so quickly I have to ask her to repeat it. She does, and I double-check it against the number the saleslady wrote down for me.

"That's the right number," I say, heart sinking. "But this isn't Johnny's."

She hangs up without saying another word. I look at Dad. A tear is glinting in the corner of his right eye from trying to hold in his laughter.

"Dad, aren't you the person who says you should never take joy in another's misfortune?"

"I'm sorry," he says, not sounding very sorry. "Call the store; the number's on the receipt. Tell them you need to change your number."

"No can do," Robby says when I explain the situation. "The system will only let us change a customer's number once every two months, and we already changed yours today."

"But what should I do if they keep calling?"

"Well, you could always learn how to make pizza!"

For a second I actually consider that. I mean, I *am* able to use the oven now.

"Sorry, kid, that wasn't very helpful. Just come back in two months, and we'll fix it. Good luck," he says, and hangs up.

Dad shakes his head. "Poor Johnny. He's missing out on a lot of orders."

"Yeah, poor Johnny," I repeat, slumping down in my seat. A minute later my phone makes an unfamiliar beep. I hold it up to look at the screen. It's my first text!

SARI SAW JAKE HARRISON
AT THE DINER!!!!!!
SWEARS SHE ALMOST FAINTED
+ HE HAD TO CATCH HER!!!!
C U 2NITE!

Sari is my most dramatic friend. She's always almost fainting over one thing or another. But for Jake Harrison I'd have fainted, too. Johnny and his pizza fly right out of my head. I text back, OMG!! WOW!, which takes me longer than expected because I keep messing up how many times I need to push each button to get the right letter. This must seriously be the last phone on earth without a real keyboard. But it doesn't matter because I'm officially In The Loop! I spend the rest of the short trip back into town fantasizing both about Jake Harrison and about how popular I'll be now that people can text me.

My warm glow of satisfaction and anticipation lasts until we pull into the restaurant parking lot and my phone rings. Dad turns off the car and we both stare at it suspiciously. "One of your friends?" he asks.

This time I pay attention to the phone number that pops up on my caller ID. I don't recognize it.

"Do you want me to answer it?" he asks.

I hand him the phone and get out of the car.

"Hello?" he says as we start walking to the restaurant. "Sorry, we're sold out of ham and pineapple pizza. Out of pizza altogether, in fact. What? Yes, I'm serious. We only sell donut holes now. No, not like the Munchkins at Dunkin' Donuts. We sell the actual *holes*. The space *inside* the donut. Right. Okay, well, good luck to you, too." He hands me back the phone. "I don't think they'll be calling again."

"Probably not," I say wearily. "Why did I want a cell phone again?"

"So your mom and I could reach you whenever we wanted."

"Oh, right, that must have been it."

Dad holds the restaurant door open for me and things get strange very fast. As usual for a Saturday night, Applebee's is packed with families and teenagers and everyone else. It just opened a few months ago, and it's the only chain restaurant allowed in Willow Falls. My theory is the town council let them in because the name reminds the old-timers of the days when apples were the main crop in town. As soon as I step through the door, my eyes light upon a half-naked Sawyer running between the tables, followed closely by our red-faced Mom, frantically waving a pair of training pants in the air. Diners are grabbing their drinks so they don't get knocked into their laps.

"Rory!" Sawyer yells gleefully when he sees me. He runs over and hugs my knees. I look up in time to see half the gymnastics team — currently the most popular girls in my grade — all texting one another and laughing. Mom's right. Texting at dinner *is* rude! I try to duck around the hostess stand in the hopes that they won't recognize me.

This probably would have worked if Sawyer wasn't hanging from my legs and chanting my name.

Then, to add to the mayhem, my phone rings. Before I can think, Sawyer lets go of my legs and snatches the phone from my hand. Mom has caught up with him by this time, but he keeps running in circles around me and she can't grab him. After pressing random buttons, he lands on the right one. "Hi, my name's Sawyer!" he says into the phone. "Pizza? I love pizza!" I try to pull the phone away, but he holds fast. "I'm naked!" he yells at the unfortunate person on the phone (and the entire restaurant, too), and then tops it off with "I have a naked butt!" I'm pretty sure that even if Mom had a buy-one-get-one-free dinner at Applebee's for the rest of her life, we won't be coming back here.

Mom and Dad team up and corner him. Dad wrenches the phone free while Mom hauls him off to the bathroom. All the while Sawyer continues to sing about his butt.

Dad hands me my phone. "Safe to say Johnny's Pizzeria has lost another loyal customer."

Chapter Five

When I wake up the next day, the lamp is turned on next to my bed. Did I leave it on all night? Why would I have done that? A bunch of disjointed images flash through my mind. Getting a phone. Losing a phone. Falling in love with a bunny. Getting another phone. Sawyer's butt streaking across a crowded restaurant filled with the popular girls from school. Annabelle giving me lessons on texting shortcuts while we eat birthday cake. Hearing Mom groan as she read over my FINALLY chart. Watching *Friday the 13th Part IX*. Oh, that's right! The movie is the reason my light is on. Even though Annabelle and I watched most of it through our fingers, I was so scared after seeing it that I was afraid to sleep in the dark. I may never sleep in the dark again.

A *ding* from my computer alerts me to a new e-mail. I scramble out of bed, throw on my glasses, and run to the desk. But it's not an e-mail — it's an IM! My first ever! Annabelle helped me set up my account last night. Mom won't need to worry about strangers IM-ing me because the only people who can write to me are kids from the school's own network. We even have to use our real name, which is really uncreative, but it's not like I'm complaining, because it's better than nothing. My first IM is from Sari, which is kind of cool, because usually we don't talk much unless Annabelle is around. Now that I can IM, I'm obviously even MORE in the loop! I sit down so quickly I almost fly backward off the chair.

Sari: Hey!! Your name popped up on the list of people who can IM now!! Wake up! I've got to tell you about my JAKE HARRISON SIGHTING!!!

Rory: This is my first IM!

Sari: Welcome to the Internet Age!

Rory: I know!!!!!!!! So what's Jake like in person?????

Sari: SOOOOOO CUTE!!! Taller than in the movies. He must have had a growth spurt. Did you hear I almost fainted?

Rory: Annabelle told me. She TEXTED me on my NEW CELL PHONE!!!

Sari: Hooray!

Rory: I know!! But I had to turn it off when I went to bed. You have no idea how many people want to order pizza at midnight!

Sari: Huh?

Rory: Never mind, long story.

Sari: Here's a picture of me with Jake!

Next to her half of the little IM box another box pops up with the word *Loading*.

Rory: You got a PICTURE with him??

Sari: Not exactly WITH him. Did it load yet?

Rory: Nope. My computer's really slow.

Sari: Do you think Jake would like it if I wore my whole collection of Hello Kitty barrettes?

Rory: I'm not sure if that's a good idea.

Sari has a thing with hair. She's always cutting hers in these weird styles or wearing really bizarre accessories. When she and Annabelle start talking hair, I tune right out. The picture finally appears, but I'm not sure what I'm looking at. I move closer to the screen. Is that a *sneaker*?

Rory: Are you sure you sent the right one? All I see is a sneaker.

Sari: That's it! That's HIS sneaker! I took it with my phone after the whole fainting thing.

Rory: LOL. Why didn't you just ask him if you could take a real picture?

Sari: I didn't want to seem like a crazed fan or something.

Rory: But you are.

Sari: I'm playing hard to get.

Rory: By fainting in his arms?

Sari: Exactly!

I'm about to argue the logic in that when Mom pokes her head in.

"On the computer already?" she asks, heading over to my desk.

Annabelle taught me what to do in these situations. I turn back to the screen and quickly write:

Rory: MOS.

Mom puts her hand on my shoulder. "I know that means *Mom over shoulder*, honey. I have a whole book on teenage Internet shorthand."

Figures.

"Tell Sari you'll type at her later. We need to go over some plans for today."

Rory: GTG. TTYL.

Sari: L8R G8R.

I can practically *hear* Mom rolling her eyes behind me. I close the IM box and spin around in my chair. "So, what do you want to talk to me about?"

Instead of responding, she pulls something shiny out of her pocket and dangles it in front of me. I eagerly hold out my hand, and she drops the silver object into it. My fingers close around it. A house key. My very own house key. I think I just grew two inches taller.

"Remember," Mom says gravely. "As President Roosevelt wisely said, 'With great power comes great responsibility.'"

"Um, wasn't that from the first issue of *Spider-Man* when Peter Parker decides to accept his fate?" Some kids know how Humpty Dumpty fell off his wall; I know how all the superheroes got their powers. Dad used to read comics to me before bed. He still would, if I didn't stop him.

Mom shakes her head. "I think it was Roosevelt."

"Rory's right," Dad calls out as he passes by in the hall.

Mom crosses her arms. "Well, whoever said it, it's still true. We're trusting you with the key because we trust that you will be responsible when you're home alone."

"Am I going to be home alone soon?" I ask, hoping I don't sound too eager.

"Not if it was up to me, but if you truly feel you're ready . . ."

"I do, I do!"

She sighs, a little dramatically if you ask me, and says, "Well, then, no time like the present."

I jump up from my chair. "Really? Now?" Images begin to swirl through my head. Dancing around my room to loud music. Eating the chocolate Mom hides behind the paper towels in the pantry. Watching whatever I want on TV. It's going to be amazing!

"Don't get too excited," Mom warns, always the mind reader. "It's only for two hours. Apparently the latest batch of *Sesame Street* puzzles were shipped without the piece containing Big Bird's head, so your father has to go sort that out, and Sawyer has a birthday party for a boy in his preschool class. We don't *have* to go, though." She frowns. "Maybe we shouldn't."

"You should, you should," I insist, leading her to the door. "I'll be fine, I promise."

She hesitates, then nods. "All right. I guess if you're going to be babysitting soon, you'll need to be able to stay home alone."

"That's true," I agree, and run off to pack Sawyer's diaper bag before she changes her mind. Down in his playroom (which used to be our dining room), I throw in two diapers, a bunch of wipes, a juice box, his chewed-up copy of *Don't Let the Pigeon Drive the Bus!*, his favorite stuffed animal (a bright pink creature of unknown gender or species that he named Hot Lips), and a change of clothes. Last, I grab a slice of pizza from the freezer, wrap it in tinfoil, and add it to the bag in case they don't serve pizza at the party. Clearly I'm going to make an excellent babysitter because I already know how to anticipate a child's every need.

Ten minutes later, I'm locking the door behind them. Mom had made me promise not to invite anyone over, not to answer the door, not to use the oven or stove, and not to play with knives. Seriously, I had to promise not to play with knives. She'd also left me the numbers of the police station, fire department, hospital, and burn unit, and made me promise to keep the home phone within reach at all times.

I wait until I hear the car scrape the bump at the end of the driveway, then spring into action. First, chocolate. Mom doesn't think anyone knows it's there, but we all do. Even Sawyer. I found him stuffing his face with Peanut M&M's one day when our parents thought he was still in his crib napping. If I ratted him out, the chocolate would be moved and I couldn't take that chance. I waited to see if Sawyer's face would swell up in reaction to the peanuts, and when it didn't, I figured all's well that ends well and stuck him back in his crib. I did suggest it was time my parents think about moving him to a bed, though, so he wouldn't climb out and hurt himself. Mom praised me for my forward-thinkingness.

No M&M's today, just Tootsie Rolls. Even though a Tootsie Roll has no actual chocolate in it, I'm willing to overlook that. Behind the candy, stuck halfway between the wall and shelf, I spot something shiny. Further investigation uncovers the bottom corner of a can of soda. I have to lean all the way into the pantry to wrestle it free. *Tab?* I've heard of that brand, but never seen it in the house before. Mom only allows soda in the house for special occasions. She probably meant to serve it with the birthday cake last night, but forgot. I guess that makes it mine! I pop it open and pour it into a tall glass with ice. It tastes like a really flat Coke.

Dad's overstuffed armchair is waiting for me and I settle in, enjoying the comfort of the soft (but not real) leather as it molds to the shape of my body. I place the glass in the convenient cup holder on the armrest and prepare to be entertained by an episode of *The Simpsons* that I'm sure aired decades ago but which I'm never allowed to watch because Mom claims it lowers IQ points.

Then I hear it. *Creak . . . creak . . . groan.* My hand freezes in midair, a Tootsie Roll halfway to my mouth. That noise sounded like it came from the house, not the TV. I hit the mute button on the remote. For almost a full minute I don't move a muscle. When I don't hear anything scarier than the gentle hum of the dishwasher, I relax back into the chair again, shaking my head. Leave it to me to freak myself out over nothing. Just as I'm about to un-mute the show, I hear *creak . . . creak . . .* and then, *slam!* Suddenly I'm a foot in the air. I have literally jumped out of my seat, nearly toppling my soda in the process. All my senses are on red alert. That was NOT my imagination! Heart pounding, I tiptoe into the hall, and peek around the corner at the front door. I can tell from here that it's still locked from the inside. That's a good sign.

Or is it? What if the intruder were smart enough to lock it behind him before he crept up the stairs to hide in my closet or under my bed?

Or what if it weren't the front door that slammed, but one of the bedroom or bathroom or closet doors? That would mean someone would have had to be in the house before my family left. But how would he have gotten around unnoticed? Unless . . . unless he's a disembodied spirit!

I run back to the family room and grab the cordless phone from where I'd left it on the coffee table. With shaky hands, I punch in Mom's cell phone number, then push myself as far into the corner of the room as my body will go.

After a few rings she picks up. Before I can say anything, I hear a muffled "No throwing Hot Lips in the car, Sawyer. That's very dangerous."

"Mom!" I whisper as loudly as I dare.

"Rory? Why are you whispering? Hold on, let me put on my hands-free." More muffled voices ensue as I wait for

Mom to find her earpiece. *Breathe*, I command myself, *just breathe*. Finally, after what feels like *forever*, she says, "Still there?"

"I'm here, I'm here!" I whisper frantically. "This might be the last time we ever speak!"

"And why's that?" she asks, not sounding particularly concerned for someone who didn't want me to stay home alone in the first place.

I cup my hand around the mouthpiece. "I heard some strange noises."

"What kind of noises?"

My eyes dart left and right. "Like creaks and a slam."

"Well, the creaks are probably just the house settling."

"Settling? Settling for what?"

"Just what an old house does. Groans and creaks sometimes."

"But our house isn't that old!" I argue. "And what about the slam?"

"Did you check the front door?"

"Yes!"

"Do you hear anything right now?" she asks.

"No," I admit.

She pauses to tell Sawyer not to kick the back of her seat. I grip the phone tighter and wonder where my mother's priorities lie. Save her only daughter from a homicidal maniac ghost, or teach Sawyer a lesson on proper car manners?

"Okay," she instructs, "go check the bathroom in the hall upstairs. Sometimes when the window's open, a strong wind sucks the bathroom door closed."

My eyes widen. "You want me to go up there alone?"

"You'll be fine. Take the phone with you."

"So I can hit him with it?"

She laughs, which wasn't the response I'd been after. "Just go check. I promise you'll be okay."

Clearly I'm more expendable than I would have hoped. "All right, I'll go. But if I don't come back, tell Sawyer he can have Throckmorton."

"I'm sure he'd like that."

I try to make my feet move, but they seem to be stuck to the carpet. "And tell Dad I'm sorry I stole a dollar from his wallet when I was eight to buy ice cream from the Good Humor man."

"You got it. Any other wrongdoings you want to confess to?"

My shoulders sag. My first twelve years have been pretty law-abiding. "No," I reply. "I guess that's it. Wait! Once when I was seven, we were driving home from Grandpa's and I pretended to be asleep when we got home so you'd carry me to bed."

"I knew you weren't sleeping."

"You did? How?"

A car honks loudly and Mom mutters something at the driver before saying, "You pulled off your glasses and put them on your night table before I laid you down. Now go upstairs already. We're only a few blocks away from the party."

"Okay, okay." I creep over to the stairs as silently as possible, cringing as my foot lands on a loose floorboard. "Still there?" I whisper into the phone.

"Still here," she assures me. I begin my climb, making sure to put very little weight on my feet to avoid more creaking. I can hear "Itsy Bitsy Spider" playing on the car's CD player. For some reason I find this comforting. What kind of ghost would want to possess my body while a nursery rhyme is being played? Then I stop short. If this were a horror movie, that's EXACTLY the kind of music they would play while the kid gets possessed!

"Mom," I hiss as I reach the top of the stairs, "can you turn the music off?" She doesn't answer. I realize from the muffled noises that she must have put the phone down to gather her stuff for the party. So much for protecting me. I guess I'm on my own. Pressing my back against the wall, I slide toward the bathroom. When I reach it, I take a deep breath and swing my head around until I'm facing the door. It's closed! I hear Mom's voice calling my name so I bring the phone back to my ear. "I'm here."

"So? Was it the bathroom door?"

"I don't know," I say, inching away. "It's closed."

"Well, open it!"

I'm about to argue about the preciousness of life, and how there's so much I haven't experienced, but then I decide to just suck it up and act my age. Before I can change my mind, I reach for the knob and swing the door open. And what do you know, a stiff breeze from an open window greets me. A huge wave of relief washes over me and I lean against the counter.

"All clear," I report.

"Good. You'll be all right?"

"I'll be fine."

"See you in a few hours."

"Thanks." We hang up, and I quickly make my way back to the family room where *The Simpsons* awaits. I take a big swig of the soda and am about to settle back in the chair when . . . *squeak, creak, groan.* It can't be the bathroom door again, since it's closed. I huddle in the chair, hug my knees, and hit the redial button. After about ten endless rings, Mom picks up. "I'm at the party, Rory, what is it?"

Now that she's on the phone, I sort of regret calling. I have to think fast. "We never, um, you know, just *talk* anymore."

No response.

I forge ahead, ignoring the sound of musical chairs in the background. "So, um, tell me about your, uh, life and stuff." I squirm as I await her reply.

"Rory?"

"Yes?" I ask meekly.

"Do you need me to come home?"

"No!" That came out sounding much more convincing than I'd expected. But if she came home now, I'd never live it down. She probably wouldn't let me babysit, either, if I can't even stay home alone in my own house in the middle of the day.

"Are you sure?" she asks.

"I'm sure. Really, I was just kidding. Have fun at the party." I hang up before I can dig myself in deeper, and pull my cell out of the pocket of my sweats. When I turn it on, the screen flashes 14 MISSED CALLS. If I hadn't turned it off, I'd have been up all night convincing people I don't sell pizza! I type a text to Annabelle, trying to remember all the texting shortcuts she went over with me.

HOW COME U DIDN'T TELL ME STAYING HOME ALONE IS SCARY? I KEEP HEARING THINGS.

<LOL. MAN UP. YOU'LL GET USED TO IT.>

DID YOU JUST TELL ME TO MAN UP? WHAT DOES THAT MEAN?

<IT MEANS STOP BEING A CHICKEN. ACT LIKE A MAN. MAN UP.>

YEAH, I DON'T KNOW ABOUT THAT.

<JUST TURN THE MUSIC UP REALLY LOUD. KEEP BUSY SO YOU DON'T THINK TOO MUCH.>

IF ANYTHING HAPPENS TO ME U CAN HAVE MY CELL PHONE.

<THAT UGLY THING? NO THANKS!>

ON BEHALF OF MY PHONE, WHO IS VERY SENSITIVE, I'D LIKE YOU TO SAY SORRY.

<QUIT TEXTING ME. GO SING INTO YOUR HAIRBRUSH OR SOMETHING.>

My thumbs are starting to cramp up, but I don't want to face the silence again.

SING INTO MY HAIRBRUSH? IS THAT WHAT YOU DO WHEN YOU'RE HOME ALONE?

<NO, BUT THAT'S WHAT THEY ALWAYS DO IN THE MOVIES.>

I THINK I'LL JUST TURN THE TV UP.

<WITH YOUR VOICE I THINK THAT'S BEST.>

She's probably right. I slip my phone back in my pocket and turn up the TV so loud that all the doors in the house could slam at the same time and I wouldn't hear them. After a few minutes, though, my brain feels like it's bouncing against my skull so I turn it off. I couldn't concentrate on Bart's antics anyway. Grabbing the bag of Tootsie Rolls, I hurry upstairs and lock myself in my bedroom. A quick check under the bed and in the closet assures me that my room, at least, is predator and ghost free. I wish I'd gone to the library last week because I don't have any new books to read, which would help take my mind off my plight. The math homework I've been putting off all weekend is staring up at me from my desk, so I give into it. But within five minutes of trying to figure out what the sizes of the other two angles would be if an isosceles triangle has one angle of ninety-six degrees, I realize that I will never encounter a time in my future when I will need to know this, whereas learning what type of food my future bunny will eat will be vital to both my future and the bunny's.

In only a few minutes online, I learn that Kyle will need daily outdoor exercise and lots of rubber toys unless I want him to chew up my sneakers and computer wires. He'll need fresh veggies and alfalfa to eat, along with rabbit pellets from the pet store. And what *I'll* need? A lot more money than I currently have, thanks to that phone insurance policy. The sooner I can start babysitting, the better.

I'm about to print out a list of *Games to Play with Your Bunny*, when an IM box pops up in the middle of the screen.

Alexa: Hi Rory! How are you?

I freeze. Alexa Montgomery is IM-ing me? ME? Alexa hasn't spoken to me since kindergarten, and even then, that was only because she thought I stole the Hershey's Kiss she'd brought in for Show and Tell. (I didn't.)

But maybe the Internet has reached across the great abyss that separates cool people like Alexa from decidedly uncool people like me. Well, here goes nothing.

Rory: Good, how are you?

As soon as I hit SEND I wish I had come up with something a little cooler than *Good, how are you*? I sound like someone's grandmother. She's probably wishing she never started this.

Alexa: I'm good too! What are you doing?

Wow! This girl must really be bored. Maybe she's home alone, too, and freaking out like me. Just because she's pretty and popular and is on the gymnastics team and has a boyfriend, doesn't mean she's not a normal person, right? So I decide to be honest.

Rory: I'm home alone for the first time. It's kind of spooky!

Her response comes quick.

Alexa: OMG, you're worse than a girl!

"Huh?" I say out loud. I reread her message a few times before it hits me. Alexa thinks she's talking to the *other* Rory. The BOY Rory. I want to crawl under my desk and die.

Alexa: I'm just kidding! I really like you, you know.

What should I do? I can't just log off, can I? But I have to admit, this bizarre turn of events is keeping my mind off of homicidal beings from beyond the grave. Might as well keep going.

Rory: I thought you had a boyfriend.

Alexa: Not since all he gave me for my birthday last month was a stupid card.

Okay, so maybe Alexa isn't the nicest girl. I sure would have been happy to get a birthday card from a boy. ANY boy. Well, anyone other than my brother, whose homemade card is currently leaking glitter all over my desk. I can't think of anything to say back, so I just wait.

Alexa: Soooo . . . do you have a girlfriend?

Is Alexa Montgomery flirting with me? I have very little (no) experience with flirting, so I'm not entirely sure.

Rory: Um, no. No girlfriend.

Alexa: Cool. Hey, did you know that at Natalie Karp's party in a few weeks, her parents aren't gonna be around after they give us lunch?

Rory: No.

Alexa: Are you going?

Rory: Yes.

Too late, I realize I probably shouldn't have said that. Boy Rory might not have been invited just because Girl Rory was.

Rory: I mean, I think I am. Unless, you know, Natalie meant to invite the other Rory instead of me.

I hold my breath to see what she'll say to this.

Alexa: What other Rory?

Figures.

Rory: You know, the girl in your grade.

Alexa: Oh! I think I know who you mean. Sort of mousy and bookish? Kind of blends into the background?

My shoulders sag.

Rory: Yeah, that's her.

Alexa: I think I saw her at Applebee's yesterday. Her brother was running around naked!

Rory: I'm sure he had a good reason.

Alexa: LOL. You're funny. But why would *she* be going to the party?

Rory: I don't know, maybe she's friends with Natalie.

Alexa: Sure, whatever you say. So . . . are you going to audition to be an extra for the movie next week? You know I was thinking . . . you sort of look like Jake Harrison.

Now even *I* can tell she's flirting. Boy Rory looks as much like Jake Harrison as *I* do! Time to end this conversation.

Rory: GTG, big test to study for.

Alexa: Cute AND smart! ☺

Rory: Um, right, thanks. Bye.

I log off before she can ask me on a *date*, and text Annabelle: ALEXA MONTGOMERY JUST THOUGHT I WAS THAT BOY RORY IN THE 7TH GRADE. SHE SAID SHE LIKES ME! I MEAN, HIM!

<OMG RU SERIOUS? HOW DID THAT HAPPEN?>

YOU FORGOT TO PUT MY LAST INITIAL AFTER MY NAME WHEN YOU SIGNED ME UP.

<OOHHHH. OOPS! SORRY!! I'LL CHANGE THAT FROM HERE. SO WHAT ELSE DID SHE SAY?>

SHE SAID AUDITIONS ARE NEXT WEEK.

<THEN WE HAVE A WEEK TO FIGURE OUT HOW TO GET PICKED!!!!!! GTG, MOM'S MAKING ME GO MAKEUP SHOPPING WITH HER. SHE SAYS I HAVE A GOOD EYE FOR COLOR.>

YOU DO.

<AW SHUCKS. BYE>

I glance over at the clock next to my bed. Less than an hour has passed since everyone left. Is that even possible? Now what do I do? The loud music idea sounds good, but the only stereo in the house is in the family room, and I'm not going back down there. I wish I had an iPod. But when I asked for one last year, Mom said, "When you're sixteen." I'm going to have to start a whole new list! By that time, iPods will be a thing of the past, and we'll probably have dime-sized implants in our ears that play music when we command it with our brains. For now, my portable CD player will have to do. I fish it out of my bottom drawer, glad to see the headset is wrapped around it and the batteries actually work.

Just sitting in my room wearing the headset feels dorky, though. I'd go for a walk outside, but I promised I wouldn't leave the house. Mom always takes a hot bath when she's stressed. I don't think I've taken one since I was seven. Bathing in the middle of the day when I'm not even dirty seems weird. But I have a whole hour to get through and an unopened bottle of bubble bath. My aunt Rachael sent it to me for my birthday, along with all these other lotions and creams that I never thought I'd use. Well, as Mom says, no time like the present. If I get electrocuted with this Discman on, I'm going to feel pretty stupid.

Careful to look both ways before stepping into the hall, I run the short distance to the bathroom and quickly lock the door behind me. Then I have to unlock it, dash down the hall to the closet for a towel, check both ways again, and dash back. Then I have to do it all over again because I forgot I had stashed the gift basket in the closet, too.

After only a few minutes luxuriating in the hot bubbles with music filling my ears, I've decided that baths are very under-rated. All my tension has drained away. My fears now seem so silly and childish. I can totally stay home alone. In fact, I am the Queen of Staying Home Alone. The bath cools off and I keep adding more hot water. I'm not sure how much time has passed, but after another CD ends and there's a brief silence in my headphones, I'm suddenly aware of activity going on outside the door. It takes my totally relaxed, hot-bath brain a few seconds to process a pounding noise. My eyes snap open. Instinct takes over. In one swift and graceful move, I fly out of the tub, send my glasses skittering across the floor, and grab my towel. Heart racing, I call out, "Who is it?" But it's too late.

A foot is already crashing through the door.

Chapter Six

They give me a choice. For one week, either no cell phone or no Internet. So now if someone IMs me, they get a message saying, *Rory cannot come to the screen. She is grounded for various reasons, including, but not restricted to, scaring her parents half to death.* At least Annabelle did as promised and fixed my screen name so I don't have to worry about Alexa or her friends receiving Mom's message. As humiliating as this is, I figure it could have been a lot worse. Apparently when Dad called to check on me and I didn't answer the house phone or my cell (both of which I'd forgotten in my room, against strict orders), he left the factory, Mom and Sawyer raced home from the party, and then when I didn't answer the pounding on the bathroom door, well, they suspected the worst. Now there's a big hole in the bathroom door and nobody is speaking to me except for Sawyer, who thought it was all very exciting.

And that can of Tab? It seems that it was stuck in the pantry when my parents moved into the house THIRTEEN YEARS AGO. They'd left it there all these years because they thought it was funny. The doctor said not to worry since I only drank one sip, but to keep an eye on me for any projectile vomiting. I'm pretty sure that wouldn't go unnoticed.

Later when Mom comes in to say good night and to see if my stomach hurts (it doesn't), I tell her again how sorry I am.

"I know you are. We just didn't know what to think. It's not so easy for us to adjust to Newly Independent Rory overnight. When we didn't hear from you, I never would have guessed you'd be taking a bath with your headphones on. That scenario wasn't included in the preteen handbook I ordered." She smiles, and I smile back, which feels nice. I feel terrible about worrying them so much.

"Do you want to check my homework?" I ask, holding the folder out to her.

She shakes her head. "Newly Independent Rory, remember? Those days are gone as of yesterday."

"Oh, right." I actually *had* remembered; I was just trying to be nice. That, and it might not hurt to get one more opinion on my geometry equations.

As she leaves, she says, "Unfortunate incident aside, you made it through your first time home alone. How does it feel?"

"It feels pretty good, unfortunate incident, you know, aside."

"You still think you're ready to babysit?"

I pause before answering. I know she's hoping I'll say no. I probably could use a few more sessions in my own house before taking on someone else's. But if I want Kyle, then I'm going to have to "man up." "Yup, I'm ready. Bring it on."

If she's disappointed, she does a good job of hiding it. "All right. You can sign up for the next Red Cross babysitting class." She kisses me on the head, and I crawl into bed. Then I realize I officially have an extra half hour on my bedtime now. A whole half hour! I can't go online due to my punishment, so I head downstairs and flick through the channels on TV. All the shows look violent or scary. I guess a half hour makes a big difference. I've had enough of being scared for one day, so I wander into the kitchen. Dad is making his sandwich for work tomorrow. When he sees me he just grunts. I guess since technically it was his foot that went through the door, he has a right to hold a grudge. At least until his foot stops hurting.

I can't help noticing that he's not making a sandwich for my lunch, too. In fact, I don't see carrot sticks or juice boxes or my blue lunch bag anywhere in sight. He might be mad at me, but I'm pretty sure he wouldn't let me starve. Unless . . . could this mean . . . I think it does! I finally get to buy my own lunch! No parents looking over my shoulder to ensure I make the healthiest choices. I reach up and give Dad a kiss on the cheek.

"What's that for?" he asks, slicing his tuna sandwich in half.

"For worrying you today."

"Well, the next time I have to kick a door down, it's coming out of your allowance."

"Deal."

I go to bed dreaming of the bags of chips and piles of warm cookies that await me in the cafeteria. I wake up groggy. It's a good thing I had picked out my outfit last night before bed, because who knows what I would come up with now. It takes until halfway through my bowl of Cheerios to feel even half awake. I guess functioning on less sleep is going to take some getting used to.

"You better hurry if you want to make it to school on time," Mom says, coming up behind me.

I turn to ask what she means and am surprised to see that she's still wearing her slippers and robe.

"Aren't you driving me?"

She shakes her head. "You walk to school now, remember?"

The last bit of sleep fog lifts. "That's right!"

"And here's your lunch money." She reaches into the pocket of her robe and hands me a five dollar bill. "I expect change."

"No problem," I say, stashing the bill in my pocket and pushing back my chair. "Well, guess I better run then."

"Guess so," she says.

I'm not sure, but I think I detect a little catch in her voice. "You're sure you don't want to drive me? I don't mind or anything."

"No, you go ahead. It's only three blocks, right? And of course you'll go directly to school, and won't talk to strangers who pull over to ask for directions, because you never know if that's really what they're after. Pretend you don't speak English or something, and walk away fast."

"But what if they really *do* need directions? Wouldn't it be rude not to help them?"

"Rory, I doubt anyone's going to ask a kid —"

"Preteen!"

"Who's going to ask a *preteen* for directions?"

"Maybe you're right. But what if they offer me candy?" I joke.

Her face grows grim. "That's not funny."

"Sorry, yeesh. I promise I won't talk to anyone. Even if old Mrs. Moody down the street comments on the weather."

"Mrs. Moody you can talk to," Mom says, closing the door behind me. Then she opens it and sticks her head out. "But make sure it's really her, and not someone masquerading as her."

Now I know where I get my paranoia from.

As I set out, it occurs to me that I'm rarely outside at this time of day. There's a crispness to the air that I never noticed just going from the house to the car, and the car to the school. The ground is still lightly covered with dew, and the air itself is filled with the smell of apples. Apples have not actually grown in Willow Falls since my grandparents' days, but I swear I smell them sometimes when the wind is right.

The walk takes longer than I would have thought, and not all the streets have sidewalks. It's amazing how many people ignore the town's pooper-scooper laws, and also what they toss in the gutters. So far I've seen numerous smashed pens, three nickels and a dime, a scratch-off lottery ticket, and two cracked CDs (Fleetwood Mac's *Rumours*, and the soundtrack to one of the *High School Musical* movies, which I know I'm supposed to like, but just don't). I think the key to this walking-to-school thing is having people to walk with. Or at least an iPod. It's not like I can wear my Discman to school with those big headphones. As I turn the last corner, a car whizzes by so close the breeze lifts the back of my hair. It comes to a stop in front of me, so I have to stop, too. Is someone seriously going to ask me for directions? Did Mom set this up as a test? I search my brain for how to say something, *anything*, in Spanish. All that comes to mind is *¿Dondé está la biblioteca?*, which means "Where is the library?" That doesn't really apply. But all that happens is the driver — an older woman — leans across the passenger seat and says, "Sorry, honey, I didn't see you."

"No problemo." And then for good measure I add, "La biblioteca." She gives me a strange look, and then sets off again. Mom would be proud.

The school yard is buzzing with activity as I approach. Usually a few kids hang out on the front steps, or where the buses let out, but now the whole school is outside, watching men and women carry big pieces of equipment from a huge truck parked in the teachers' lot. As I get closer, I see a bunch of smaller trailers, too. My pace quickens as I realize what's going on. The movie people are setting up!

I spot Annabelle and Sari next to one of the trailers and run over to them.

"Hey, you made it!" Annabelle exclaims.

"Why wouldn't I?"

"It's not every day your dad has to break a door down to rescue you from drowning in the tub!"

She and Sari laugh.

"For your information, he didn't break the door down. He just kicked a hole through it."

"I hope he was wearing a shoe!" Sari says, and this cracks them up even more.

"And I wasn't drowning," I mutter. When they finally stop laughing, I ask, "So what's going on here?"

"This one is hair and makeup!" Annabelle says, pointing to the nearest trailer. "We've been trying to look inside, but the windows are too high."

We all jump up, but she's right, still a foot too high. "What if we get a box or something to stand on?" Sari suggests.

"Good idea," Annabelle says, looking around. Before we find anything useful, the bell rings, and hordes of kids start running for the door. The morning announcements are all about the movie. The principal warns everyone to stay away from the trailers and not to approach the crew or the actors, or *there will be serious consequences*. She explains that the crew is here this week to set up the lights and other equipment, and for the director to block scenes. This means we're supposed to be careful when we see big pieces of black tape on the hallways, or thick wires running along the walls and ground. She thanks us all for our patience and cooperation. Almost as an afterthought, she tells us that auditions for extras will be held next Monday. Squeals reverberate through the halls. I hear a phone beep, and it takes me a few seconds to realize it's mine! Luckily there was so much noise that Mrs. Foley didn't hear it. They have a very strict No Texting rule in school, even though everyone does it anyway. I slide the phone out of my pocket and look down. It's a text from Annabelle, whose bio class is on the other end of the building.

<WE HAVE TO GET TO THE MALL THIS WEEK TO PREPARE. MAKEUP STORE & A CUTE OUTFIT THAT WE CAN ALSO WEAR TO NAT'S PARTY.>

I slip the phone back in my pocket, feeling pretty pleased with myself about receiving my first in-school text. Then right as Mrs. Foley asks for our geometry homework, my phone rings. LOUD. SOOOOO LOUD. Why hadn't I put it on vibe after Annabelle's text? My phone doesn't have cool ringtones like other phones, or an option to play a real song. All it has is a really annoying series of rings. I am horrified. I haven't figured out yet how to send calls to voice mail, so it just keeps going.

"I'm really sorry," I call out over the sound. "My mom told me to always keep it on. I meant to put it on vibe."

Mrs. Foley's hands are on her hips. "Well, Ms. Swenson. Aren't you going to answer it?"

The class giggles.

"That's okay," I insist. "I don't need to."

"It might be important," she says.

I know she doesn't really think that. I've heard this conversation before, when Leo Fitzpatrick forgot to turn off his phone last month. At least he got the last word by writing a pretty funny poem about it for the school paper. I'm no poet, though. Leo flashes me a sympathetic look from two desks down.

I fumble with the phone, open it, and say hello. With everyone's eyes on me, I sink low into my chair. "No, this isn't Johnny's Pizzeria. You have the wrong number."

Well, that pretty much brings down the house. Even Mrs. Foley can't suppress a chuckle at my pain. "All right, everyone, settle down," she says. "I think Ms. Swenson learned her lesson, so I'm going to let her keep her phone today. But you only get one warning."

I nod and quickly set it to vibe. Mom and I need to have a talk.

In the hall between classes, kids keep coming up to me asking for pizza. Some of them weren't even in my class! I wonder who was secretly texting under their desks.

In the hour since school started, the film crew has really jumped right in. Thick black extension cords line both sides of the halls, running directly under the lockers, and then up and around the classroom doors. At the far end of the hall, a guy is standing on a tall ladder attaching a huge round light to the ceiling. I watch him for a minute, half-aware of a boy's voice behind me asking someone for directions to class. Then two girls laugh and tell him it's on the third floor. Our school doesn't have a third floor. While I watch, the man on the ladder leans over and suddenly the brightest light I've ever seen floods the hallway. And then I can't see anything. I stumble backward, and would have hit the lockers if I hadn't hit the lost boy first. All up and down the hall people are yelling and bumping into things.

"Hey, are you all right?" the boy asks, straightening me up.

I rub my eyes and turn to look at him. All I can see are the outer edges of his face and body. I close my eyes and open them again.

"Maybe you should go to the nurse's office. If you tell me where it is, I'll take you there."

As he speaks, his features start getting more defined. I close my eyes for a few seconds, and try again. Much better. "I think I'm okay, thanks."

"Strange goings-on at this school," the boy says. He looks young, so he must be a new fifth grader.

I've never heard anyone say "goings-on" before. "It's not usually like this." I gesture around to the power cords and the other kids recovering from their near-blindness.

"SORRY 'BOUT THAT, EVERYONE!" the guy on the ladder yells out above our heads. "DIDN'T REALIZE IT WAS SET TO MAX!"

"Do you need help finding your class?" I ask the boy.

"Can you point me to the stairs to the third floor?"

I shake my head. "There is no third floor."

His face falls. "Oh."

"Here, let's see." I lean over and look at his schedule. "Room 108. Ah, that's a tricky one because the rooms don't go in order on that wing. That's probably why you couldn't find it."

"Like I said, strange school." He smiles at me, and I'm glad to see he's cheered up a bit.

"C'mon, I'll take you there."

"You'll be late," he points out a second before the bell rings.

"That's okay. I'll just blame it on the temporary blindness thing." Which is exactly what I have to do five minutes later when my science teacher, Mr. Collins, asks me why I'm late. It leads to a whole lecture on how a bright flash of light "bleaches" an image, and we can't see anything. Over a short time, the rods and cones can resume sending the message through retinal nerve fibers to the optic nerve and brain. I sure hope we're not going to get tested on that. It helps my case when the principal comes on the loudspeaker to apologize for any student inconvenienced by the bright light and promises that the crew will be more careful in the future.

When I get to the cafeteria for lunch, the line to buy food snakes almost to the doorway. Why have I never noticed that before? I stand at the end of it, wishing I'd left my heavy book bag in my locker, and scan the line for Annabelle and Sari. When I don't see them, I look over to our usual table, and there they are, already eating from their trays. Annabelle catches my eye, says something to Sari, and heads over.

"How did you get your food so fast?" I ask. "This line looks like it takes forever."

"Oh, we have a whole system worked out," Annabelle explains. "Most people go to their locker before lunch, but I run right here from gym and get on line. Sari's English class is right down the hall, so she gets here just before me, usually. Otherwise you could stand on this line till the bell rings."

"Yeah, I see that."

"Do you want me to wait with you?"

I glance back at the table. Sari is hunched over her tray, not looking at anyone. "No, that's okay. I think Sari needs you."

"You've got your money?"

I nod and hold out my five dollar bill.

"You could buy one of everything with that much," she says. "Not that you'd want to, trust me. We'll eat slow, don't worry."

When she's gone, I immediately wish I'd given her my bag to bring back to the table. No one else on line has theirs.

The line moves forward very slowly, but it does move. The smell of unidentifiable food gets stronger. "First time?" the boy ahead of me asks, glancing at my bag and my clutched five dollar bill. I look up in surprise to see Leo Fitzpatrick. Usually the kids at school don't just randomly start talking to me. It's that whole mousy, bookish thing. But Leo always has a smile for everyone. I know before I even look that Amanda Ellerby will be standing next to him. The two of them are practically inseparable, but not in a dating sort of way, at least I don't think so. They got into a huge fight a couple of years ago and weren't talking for like a year, but they both have the same birthday, and last year on their birthday something happened that brought them back together. Neither of them will tell anyone what it was, though. It's like the town's big mystery, which says a lot about how exciting life in Willow Falls is.

"Yeah, I'm usually a brown bagger," I reply. "Does it show?"

He nods. "The heavy book bag on your shoulder, the money already out, the shifting of the weight from foot to foot, the heavy sighing."

I laugh. "Oh."

"Hey," Amanda says, "I heard about your phone ringing in class."

I notice she has a pair of drumsticks sticking out of her back pocket and wonder how they don't break when she sits down.

Leo reddens. "Sorry, I just told her because, you know, the same thing had happened to me. Well, not the part about the pizza."

"That's okay. At least it's given people something else to talk about besides my three-year-old brother running around Applebee's half-naked."

"That was YOUR brother?" Amanda gasps, then covers her mouth. "Sorry! My friend Stephanie was there and she told me about it."

We both instinctively look toward the table where Stephanie, Alexa, Mena, and the rest of the gymnastics team sit. Amanda and I have never had any classes together, so I don't know her very well. But I think it's cool that she plays the drums and hangs out with Leo when she could be sitting at the popular table. I bet banging on the drums releases a lot of aggression.

"It's okay," I assure her. "At least no one put up a video on the Internet. I hope!"

"So why today?" Leo asks. "You heard they're serving Sloppy Joe Surprise and couldn't wait to see what the surprise would turn out to be?"

I smile. "This is going to sound weird . . ." I trail off, unsure if I want to tell them about my list. But I'm enjoying talking to them, and usually people don't go out of their way to talk to me.

"Believe me," Amanda says, sharing a glance with Leo. "Nothing sounds weird to us."

"Well, I sort of have this list of things I'm allowed to do now that I'm twelve. Buying lunch is one of them. I know that sounds stupid. I mean, I've heard what they say about school lunches."

"No, I get it," Leo says. "It's like a rite of passage, something you have to do to mark getting older."

"So how's it going?" Amanda asks. "The list, I mean."

"It's been . . . interesting." I'm spared from saying anything else because we've actually made it to the pile of green plastic trays. Leo takes the one on top and hands it back to me.

"Is it supposed to be wet?" I ask, wiping my hand on my jeans.

"They're always wet," Leo confirms. "Makes it that much more fun trying to keep your food from sliding off."

I check out the scene. Three elderly ladies in hairnets lined up behind the counter. Soda and juice on refrigerated shelves behind us. Chips and cookies in baskets at the end. When it's our turn to order, Amanda whispers, "Don't take anything from that one; she always gives the smallest portions."

I follow her gaze to the last woman in the row, the shortest and stockiest. Although she's currently facing away from me, dropping a tiny scoop of tuna onto a kid's plate, I gasp with recognition. As I whirl around to tell them I know her from the Reservoir, my book bag swings behind me, knocking a seventh grade girl's food completely off her tray and sending it clattering to the floor. She stands there, staring down at the floor, the soda she had just grabbed from the shelf now dangling from her hand.

"Omigod, I'm so sorry," I say, bending down to help her pick things up. There's nothing to be done about the sloppy joe, though. It's a huge mess of ground beef, chunks of what I hope are onion but could be anything, and red sauce. A lot of red sauce.

"Don't worry," Leo says, hurrying over and placing a few layers of napkins on top of the mess. "Happens all the time." I look up to see that the lunch lady is already replacing the girl's sandwich. I hope the sauce on the side of her shoe won't stain. By the time I collect myself enough to look for the short, white-haired woman, she's gone.

"Where is she?" I ask, looking in all directions. "Where'd she go?"

"Must be her lunch break," Amanda says with a shrug. She points at the food counter. "It's your turn."

After seeing the sloppy joe in all its glory on the floor, I point to a turkey sandwich. The woman plops it onto my plate along with some mashed potatoes. I follow Amanda and Leo down the line, sliding my tray along like they do.

"Did you guys ever notice anything strange about that lunch lady? The one you pointed out to me?"

"Strange like what?" Leo asks, pulling a hot pretzel out of the case.

I take a pretzel, too. "Like if she has a strange birthmark on her cheek? Kind of looks like a duck?"

"I never noticed anything like that," Amanda says, grabbing some milk. "Have you, Leo?"

Their eyes meet for a split second before Leo shakes his head. "Nope."

"I'm sure I know her," I mumble as I hand over my five dollars to the cashier. She hands me back two.

"Enjoy your lunch," Leo says, as he and Amanda head off in the other direction.

But all I can think is, *You won't get what you want, until you see what you need.* What is it I need to see? And will I know it when I see it?

Chapter Seven

After school, Annabelle, Sari, and I had planned to scope out the trailers to see if we could find which one has Jake Harrison's name on it. But to my surprise, Mom is waiting for me behind the row of buses, leaning against the door of her car, texting. From a distance, my mom doesn't look that much different from a teenager, but still, it's embarrassing. I tell Annabelle and Sari to go without me, then hurry over to her, assessing the situation as I go. The fact that she's standing outside her car means she doesn't have Sawyer. If something were wrong, she'd be frantically yelling into the phone, not casually texting. So why is she here?

I dig out my house key (now attached to a really cool silver key chain with the number "12" on it from Sari) and wave it in the air. "Did you forget I'm allowed to walk home on my own?"

She presses a few more buttons on her phone, then slips it into her pocket. "No, I didn't forget. I thought I'd swing by and take you on an errand with me while Sawyer's on a playdate."

"An errand?" I repeat, staring longingly after Annabelle and Sari, who I can see have already dodged the security guard posted at the end of the parking lot.

"C'mon," she says, opening the passenger door for me. "You'll like this one."

As we maneuver around the buses, Mom asks, "So, what did you buy for lunch today?"

I tick things off on my fingers. "Turkey sandwich, mashed potatoes, juice, and a hot pretzel." Now, had she asked what I *ate* for lunch instead of what I *bought*, I would have been forced to admit that all I ate was the hot pretzel.

"Those sound like good choices."

"Actually . . . they didn't taste very good." I wait for her to say she'll go back to making my lunch, but she doesn't. As we turn onto Main Street, my phone vibrates. It had been going off all day, which was very distracting. I answer it, tell them they have the wrong number, and hang up. "Mom, you have to let me turn off my phone during the day. The pizza people call, like, every five minutes. It almost got taken away this morning."

"I'll think about it," she says. I've just put it away when a buzz alerts me to a new text. That could only mean one thing.

<WE FOUND HIS TRAILER!!!!!!!>

Why do I miss all the fun things? I stare out the window glumly until Mom makes a left into the bank parking lot. I perk up. The errand I'm supposedly going to like is at the bank? Is she going to give me the money for my bunny? Seems unlikely, but why else would we be here?

She leads me inside and surprises me further by telling the bank clerk we need to access our safe-deposit box. I didn't even know we *had* a safe-deposit box. What else don't I know about my parents' secret lives? This is all very mysterious. The clerk asks if my mom has her key, and she says yes. Then he grabs a huge set of keys hanging off a round wire chain and motions for us to follow him. I had hoped we'd be going into the vault, because that's how it always is in the movies, but we pass right by the huge gold-colored door with the wheel on the outside. He unlocks a door at the end of a short hallway, and we follow him inside. This is a little more what I had expected to see.

Rows and rows of boxes along the wall that look like the boxes at the post office in town, except these each have two keyholes. As the guy begins flipping through the keys on his chain, my phone vibrates loud enough to be heard. Mom glances at me and says, "Boy, that really does go off a lot, doesn't it?"

I nod vigorously.

"Must be a pain."

Again with the vigorous nodding.

The guy holds up the key that matches my mom's box number and says, "Ready?" They both stick their keys in the holes and turn them at the exact same time. The door springs open and Mom slides out a narrow metal box. The guy directs us over to an area in the back with private booths, and tells us to hit the buzzer by the door when we're ready to leave.

My curiosity is at an all-time high. Gold bars? Fake passports? Stacks of hundred dollar bills tied together with twine? The booth has a small table with a velvet pad covering half of it, and a curtain that Mom pulls shut behind us. We sit on the small bench and I don't take my eyes off the box as Mom flips open the lid. At first all I see are papers with words like *Deed*, *Homeowners Insurance*, *Last Will and Testament*. Mom quickly lifts these out and places them to the side. Underneath are a few silk pouches of different sizes. Not as exciting as my initial guesses, but still intriguing. "What are those?" I ask.

She takes out the largest one and empties it onto the velvet pad. My eyes widen as jewelry of all sizes and shapes tumbles out. Necklaces, earrings, bracelets, rings with stones of various colors and shapes, some the size of grapes! The only jewelry I've ever seen Mom wear is her wedding ring, dainty little earrings, and maybe a bracelet or two if she and Dad are going out.

I can't help reaching out to touch the pile. "What *is* all this? Did you rob a jewelry store?"

She laughs. "Nothing that sinister. I inherited this from your grandmother and great-grandmother. You'll inherit it from me one day."

I grab her arm. "You're dying? Is that why you brought me here?"

She laughs. "I'm not dying, I promise!"

When I calm down enough, I pick through the different pieces. Everything is so . . . *big*. "How come you never wear any of this?"

"It's not really my style," she says, scooping it up and putting it back in the pouch. "Tastes were different back then."

"It's really cool and everything, but why did you want to show it to me?"

She reaches for one of the smaller pouches, a deep red rose–colored one. "This is what I want to show you. Actually," she says, placing the pouch in my hand, "I want to give it to you. It's from your grandmother. For when you turned twelve."

My eyes instantly sting with tears, and I'm not a big crier. I only have a few memories of my mother's mom, who died when I was four. Grandma was still really young when it happened, and I remember Mom cried for weeks. It probably didn't help that I couldn't understand and kept asking where Grandma was.

I bounce the small pouch a bit in my hand. It feels so light, almost like it's empty. After seeing the pile of jewelry from the other pouch, I'm a little nervous about opening it. What if I don't like it? I wouldn't want to make Mom feel bad. I slowly pull open the drawstring and turn the bag over onto the velvet pad like I'd seen her do. Out fall two delicate gold earrings, each with a circle of tiny diamonds surrounding a deep green stone.

"Those are emeralds," Mom says as I pick one up for a closer look. "They'll bring out the green of your eyes."

"They're beautiful," I say in a hushed tone. "They're really for me?"

"Yup. Do you remember them?"

I look up at her in surprise. "Should I?"

"Probably not, but you actually picked them out."

"I did?"

"When you were three. You came with me to pick out a birthday gift for Grandma, and these are what you chose."

I spin the earring so the stones glint in the light. "Wow, I had good taste at three!"

"How about on Saturday we go get your ears pierced? That way you'll be able to wear them to Natalie's party in a few weeks, if you want."

I turn and give my Mom a big hug, something I haven't spontaneously done in I don't remember how long.

"Hey, don't thank me, thank Grandma."

I rest the pouch on my lap for the whole ride home, and then run up to the bathroom to hold the earrings up to my ears. They'll show off my eyes a lot better without my glasses. Once I get my contact lenses and my ears pierced and Annabelle and I go to the makeup store, people might stop mistaking me for Boy Rory. And if they don't, that may say more about *him* than me!

Since I'm only on Day Two of my IM ban, I try to stay off the computer so I'm not tempted. I debate going downstairs to say hi to Dad when he comes home from work. Mom told me he had to wear a slipper to work today due to the swelling in his foot, so he probably isn't in the mood to see me.

Instead I busy myself by cleaning my room, which, even though I boxed up most of its contents, has somehow managed to get messy again. I pick up my FINALLY chart and admire it. I've already worked my way through a lot of the Small (but still Very Important and Worthwhile) Things, and some of the Big Things, too, with more to follow in the next few days. Exciting! When I try to lean it back against the wall, it flops over, revealing the phone chart I had made while all hyped up on caffeine. I read it over, proud of the thorough job I did. Then my eyes light upon the following line: *Parental control over which phone numbers I can accept calls from.* My eyes widen. Is that the phone I wound up with? I had been so thrilled just to hear my parents say I could get one of the choices, that I had completely forgotten which special features went with which phone. Plus I'd hoped they'd never want to use that option, so I must have blocked it from my mind. I grab my phone and hold it up to the chart, reading the make and model number. Yup! It's the same one!

I throw open my bottom desk drawer and pull out the phone manual, which I'd tossed in there without even glancing at. Clutching it to my chest, I run downstairs. My parents and Sawyer are in the family room watching *Elmo's Potty Time* on DVD. Personally I think my parents are wasting their time. The kid is just not interested.

"Guess what?" I announce, standing directly in front of the TV.

"RORY!" they all shout.

"Okay, okay." I scoot out of the way before Sawyer can miss the all-important lesson on where toilet paper comes from. "But this is important," I insist, holding up my phone. "Did you know that you can fix it so only you and my friends can call me and none of those pizza calls get through?"

"Yes," they reply.

When I can close my jaw, I ask, "You knew that?"

"Sure we knew it," Dad says. "You told us in your presentation."

My arms fall to my sides. "Why didn't you tell me?"

"It's your phone," Mom says with a shrug. "Your phone, your responsibility, remember?"

I open my mouth, sputter for a few seconds, and shut it again. I'm tempted to say *never mind*, but I'm really tired of explaining why I will not be there in thirty minutes or less with their pizza. "Here," I say, placing the phone and the manual on the couch next to them. "You know Annabelle's and Sari's numbers."

I start to storm out of the room in what I hope is frustrated defiance, when Dad calls out, "Are you sure those are the only ones you want to get through? No one else from school?" I hear Mom give him a curt "Shh!" and he calls, "Never mind." But of course it's too late. He has effectively reminded me I have very few close friends. But Mom doesn't need to protect me from this fact. It really doesn't bother me that much. After all, I'll soon have my bunny. And they don't call a rabbit a girl's best friend for nothing. Or wait, maybe that's a diamond. Well, I have those, now, too!

Later, while I'm brushing my teeth, Mom hands me a piece of paper. I wipe my mouth and hold it up. It's an announcement for the Red Cross babysitting class.

"I looked it up online and printed it out," she says, then points to the bottom of it. "The next class in town is on Saturday, and then there isn't another one for two months."

"Can you take me on Saturday, then?"

"Okay, I'll give them a call and sign you up. We'll do the ear piercing the following week." She takes the flyer and closes the bathroom door behind her.

It's so hard to figure Mom out. Sometimes she can be so nice to me, and sometimes she makes everything harder.

. . . .

I'm pretty sure the principal's promise to the parents that the movie wouldn't disrupt our classroom activities was a bold-faced lie. Besides all the technical equipment like the lights, sound boards, camera stands, and power cords, the film crew needs to "modify" a few things around the school. So all week we've had to watch out for fresh paint, piles of wooden planks, sheets of metal, toolboxes, various assorted "props" like fake posters advertising fake school dances, and cardboard cutouts of the actors that will supposedly be used as stand-ins to test the lighting and camera angles.

Actually, the cardboard cutouts are pretty cool. Someone drew a heart on the one for Jake. My money's on Sari. The only bad thing about them is that now we know that Jake's real life on-again off-again girlfriend, Madison Waters, is going to be in the movie, too. We've decided to hold an emergency meeting about it at lunch. Having learned that my history class is too far from the cafeteria to get me there in time to meet Annabelle or Sari on line, I've taken to giving one of them my lunch money in the morning and having them choose for me. Some days have been better than others. One day I ate only potato chips because I couldn't make it through the crunchy pasta. Today it's Frankfurter Friday, and I figure it's hard to mess up a hot dog.

The conversation is already in full swing when I arrive.

"I heard they're *pre-engaged*," Sari shrieks, eyes blazing. "At fourteen! She wears a little gold promise ring!"

Annabelle drops her fork and it clatters on the table. "Are you *serious*?"

"No way!" I pull my tray toward me.

Sari nods, and slumps in her seat in despair. We stare at our food and contemplate this announcement. Then I shrug and bite into my hot dog. If Jake Harrison and Madison Waters have found true love together, then good for them.

After a few chews I reach for my juice and guzzle half of it. Turns out you *can* mess up a hot dog. Fortunately I have a hot pretzel to turn to. Annabelle and Sari spend the rest of the period deciding if we should still try to sneak into Jake's trailer next week or not, and decide we should. Right before the bell rings, Annabelle and I make plans to meet at the babysitting class tomorrow. Sari can't go because she won't be twelve till next month and that's the minimum age for the class. Plus she's not really the babysitting type. I'm not sure Annabelle is, either, but she'll do anything to escape a house of five boys (with their assorted friends, girlfriends, and teammates) on the weekends.

Annabelle's mom picks me up at noon and drives us to the Willow Falls Community Center, where the class is being held. It starts at 12:30 and goes till 5:00. That's a lot of stuff to learn! If my mom had driven us, she would have insisted on coming in and escorting us to the right room. Annabelle's mom just waves, tells us to have fun and learn a lot, and drives off to the mall. Apparently she doesn't want to be home with all those boys, either.

The main room of the community center is slowly filling with senior citizens, who, by the look of the square tables, stacks of cards, and plastic poker chips being set up, are settling in for some serious betting. Signs direct us to follow the long hallway till the end. On our way, we pass a bunch of small rooms. The first one is a day care center, surprisingly full of little kids for a Saturday. Next to that, an aerobics class is in full swing, which might explain the full day care center. Competing with the disco beat is this low chanting sound coming from a room across the hall. We exchange a look and rush over to peek. David Goldberg, a kid in my math class, is standing up behind a little wooden podium, reading in what I quickly identify as Hebrew.

"Practicing for his Bar Mitzvah," I whisper to Annabelle. "I heard him talking about it in class." He's not too bad, even though his voice cracks on every third word. Annabelle wants to stay and listen, but I say, "Hey, what's the first rule of being a good babysitter?"

"Bring candy to bribe the kids into being good?"

"No! It's to be prompt so you don't hold up the parents who are trying to leave. So we should be prompt for the class, too."

"Wow, you really *are* going to be a great babysitter," she says, hurrying alongside me.

"I know."

It's easy to tell when we've reached the right room, because ten other girls (and two boys) our age are sitting at big round tables covered with things like first aid kits, fake babies with fake diapers, board games, and boxes of microwavable macaroni and cheese. This is definitely going to be an interesting four and a half hours.

The teacher, a woman in her forties or fifties with a no-nonsense blunt haircut and a very efficient manner, has us go around the tables and introduce ourselves and say what kind of babysitting experience we've had. The last girl to go is the only one I don't know from school. She looks very young and I wonder if she's in a lower grade. "My name's Kira," she says. Her voice is very soft. "My family just moved here last week. I have two younger brothers. Usually my older sister or brother takes care of them, but it's going to be my turn soon."

I can't tell if she's happy about this or not. The teacher checks her name off the list, then hesitates. "You *are* twelve, right?"

Kira nods, blushing slightly.

"Okay, then," she says, laying her attendance sheet on the counter. "My name is Rosemary, and I'll be your guide for the afternoon. By the time you leave today, you'll have learned how to be safe and responsible babysitters who get asked back by your clients. Our class will be divided into three sections." She holds up one finger. "First, ensuring a safe and healthy environment." Another finger goes up. "Second, caring for the younger child, newborn through age five. And last, we'll learn how to handle the older child. Between each section we'll have a fifteen-minute break."

Out of the corner of my eye I can see that Annabelle has already drifted. She's admiring her nails (each one recently painted a different pastel color). I give her a little kick and she straightens up.

"But before we begin," Rosemary says, "we need to talk about something that weighs heavily on the mind of every young babysitter."

She lets her words hang in the air. When no one volunteers anything, she takes a deep breath and announces, "Death!"

Fourteen pairs of eyes widen. Did she just say *death*?

She starts pacing. "The leading cause of death for a child under seven is household accidents." She starts counting on her fingers again. "Bites, stings, burns, choking, strangulation, drowning, falls, fires, poisoning, injuries from toys, blood loss from wounds. And who could forget that silent killer, carbon monoxide!"

Me! I want to yell. *I* could forget that. I'd like to forget that now. And all those other things, too! The rest of the class is stunned into silence as well, no doubt also wondering if they were cut out to be babysitters after all. And to think, she didn't even mention home intruders or ghosts!

Annabelle raises her hand. Rosemary leans over to check her attendance list. "Yes, Annabelle?"

"I thought babysitting was supposed to be fun."

"It *is* fun," Rosemary assures us. "As long as everyone takes the job seriously. And your main job is to ensure the safety and security of the children you are watching."

Annabelle is not so easily put off. "But how can I have a good time if I'm worried that any second some kid could fall down the stairs and crack his head open?"

Rosemary's lips form a straight line. Then she says, "Well, hopefully you will have put in place the proper safety protocols to prevent that from happening. That's why you're all here today."

Before Annabelle can interrupt further, Rosemary picks up an armload of paperback books. She walks through the room, placing one in front of each of us. "This is your Babysitter's Training Handbook. It is your new bible. Read it carefully, cover to cover, before beginning your first assignment. It will teach you how to instantly recognize a hazardous situation and how to defuse it. It will teach you basic first aid skills and how to handle various emergencies. The book goes into more depth than we'll be able to in these few hours."

"When does the fun come in," Annabelle mutters.

Rosemary raises her voice. "Of course, it also covers topics like appropriate games to play at each age level, preparing healthy meals and snacks, and how to set up a smooth and easy bath and bedtime routine."

By the time the first break comes, I have learned how to dress a wound, wash out an eye, tell the difference between first-, second-, and third-degree burns, and perform CPR without (hopefully) cracking any ribs or causing the child's lungs to explode. I actually *do* feel more confident in case something unexpected happens. But considering how many bathroom breaks Annabelle has taken, I think she's second-guessing the way she's chosen to spend the day.

I spend most of the break sipping from the cup of grape juice Rosemary gave each of us, and watching the other kids talking. The only other person not talking to anyone else is the new girl, Kira. She has her face buried in a book, her dark hair streaming over it. I wish I had thought to bring a book. I'm always curious what other people are reading, so I can't help peering over her shoulder as I cross the room for a juice refill.

At first glance I see photographs, not words, and assume it's a photo album of her family, or maybe the friends she left in her old hometown. Her face appears in almost all the pictures. But at second glance, my brain registers another familiar face. JAKE HARRISON is in Kira's photo album! With *her*! On a ski slope! In a pool! On the red carpet at a movie premiere!

I must make some kind of squeal or gasp, because she jerks her head up and then fumbles to close the album. I can't help it; my eyes are bugging out of their sockets. They simply will not return to their regular size. "How . . . where . . ." I fumble for the right words but they don't come.

"It's not what you think," she whispers. "They're not real."

My brow crinkles and I move to sit down in the empty seat next to her. "Not real? What do you mean?"

With a glance around to make sure no one's listening, she creaks the album back open and I eagerly lean closer. Now that I'm a few inches away instead of a few feet, I can see that while it's Kira's face all right, it has been carefully cut out of another picture and pasted over some other girl's body, most likely Madison Waters's. And the pictures aren't really photographs, they're cut out from magazines. Even up close, I can tell a lot of attention and concentration went into making sure everything lined up perfectly. It is very impressive, really.

"I know it's really stupid. . . ." she says, lowering her head so I can't see her eyes anymore.

I assure her it's very cool and not stupid at all. I think she says thanks, but her voice is so soft it's hard to tell for sure. Rosemary announces break is over, so I push back my chair to go. This time I clearly hear her say, "Don't tell anyone, okay?"

I make the lock-my-lips-and-throw-away-the-key gesture and return to my table. Annabelle is busy texting and doesn't look up right away. This is good since it will allow the shock that's probably still on my face to fade a little.

"Sari says hi," Annabelle reports, slipping her phone into her bag just as Rosemary plops a baby boy doll in front of her. "Thanks," Annabelle says brightly, picking up the baby by his leg. Rosemary places a girl baby in front of me, which I'm glad about. I know all I ever need to know about a boy baby's anatomy and the diapering challenges that come with it.

For the next hour we diaper, dress, undress, swaddle, rock, feed, and sing to our babies. We practice playing LEGOs with imaginary toddlers, read to them, and take turns using the microwave to prepare mac 'n' cheese. The two boys in the class were a little uncomfortable at first, but they really got into making LEGO castles. I think if I were a little boy, having an older boy as a babysitter would be cool.

Halfway through the next break, my cell phone goes off. I hadn't set it on vibe this morning, figuring only four people can call me now, all of whom know where I am. I pull the phone out of my bag and see our home number flashing on the screen.

"Hello? Should I be worried?"

"Nope," Mom replies. "You should be thanking me."

I take the phone out into the hall. Annabelle follows, texting Sari again.

"Why should I be thanking you?"

"Because I just got you your first gig!"

"My first gig?" I repeat.

"Your first babysitting job!" she says. "Annabelle's mother is going to pick you girls up fifteen minutes early and bring you right home so you can prepare."

"But . . . but I haven't had time to read the manual," I argue.

"So you'll bring it with you and if there's a problem, you can just look it up."

I guess I can't argue with the logic of that.

"You're the one who said you're ready to start making money, right?"

"I do, I want the job. It's just . . ."

I look up to see Annabelle hopping around the hall with her fingers crooked behind her head like bunny ears. I have to laugh.

"Okay, Mom. Tell them I'll do it." Anything to get Kyle sooner.

"Will do," she says, hanging up.

Annabelle hops a few more times, scrunches her nose up and down, then asks, "So who are you babysitting for?"

I pause. "I have no idea."

As we head back into the room, she says, "I hope it's not the Harris twins down the block from you. I heard they set their last babysitter's hair on fire."

I explain the situation to Rosemary, and she gives me and Annabelle some forms to take home with us that she'd normally give out at the end of class. "Bring this one with you tonight," she instructs me. "It's for the family to fill out — information about the child, any special needs, phone numbers, house rules, things like that." I promise I'll bring it.

Annabelle and I have to leave right in the middle of a lecture about not letting older kids manipulate you into breaking their parents' rules. The rest of the rooms off the long hall are empty now, but the senior citizens are still going strong, bets flying left and right as we enter the main room.

"Isn't that Leo and Amanda from school?" Annabelle asks, pointing to the couches in the back of the room. I look over, and sure enough, it's them. They're talking and laughing with a group of old men. From their ease on the couch, I'd guess they come here regularly.

"Should we go say hi?" I ask. I usually defer to Annabelle for social protocol.

She shakes her head. "My mom's waiting outside. And you don't want to be late tonight. The whole promptness thing and all."

I glance back at them one last time, and just as I do, Amanda looks up and meets my eyes. And then, I swear, she winks! Why would Amanda Ellerby wink at me?

"C'mon," Annabelle says, pulling me out the door. "I'd like to salvage some sunlight today. I'm getting paler by the second." I let her pull me, but when I take one last look, Amanda is engaged in conversation as though she never saw me.

Chapter Eight

I let myself into the house with my key — a small task, but one that still makes me a little giddy — and quickly locate Mom in Sawyer's playroom, playing with Play-Doh. "It's not the Harris twins, is it?"

She shakes her head. "You'll be babysitting for Emily St. Claire. I'm sure you remember her mother from my book club."

"I guess so." I don't want to admit that all her book club friends are kind of interchangeable. I only see them once every few months when the meeting is at our house, and Sawyer and I usually get shooed away pretty quickly. I don't think much book talk gets done what with all the food and wine they go through.

"Look, Rory," Sawyer says, holding up a blob of purple Play-Doh. "I made a horsey!"

"That's great, Sawyer!" I say, bending down to ruffle his hair.

"Wanna play?" he asks.

I shake my head. "I have to play Play-Doh with someone else tonight."

Mom pulls some purple horsey from the tips of her hair and says, "I think Emily is too old for Play-Doh."

"Really?" I had pictured a really little kid for some reason. "How old *is* she?"

"Ten, I think."

"Ten! She's only two years younger than me?"

Mom nods. "Is that a problem?"

"It's just . . . weird. I mean, isn't it?"

"It doesn't have to be. I thought it would be a good way to break you into the whole thing. No diapering, no reading books to her for hours on end."

I have to admit that's true. "But what if she won't listen to me?"

"You could have that problem at any age," she replies. "But don't worry, she's a lovely child. She's always very helpful when the club meets at their house. I left some pasta for you in the kitchen; then get changed and I'll drive you over there a little before six."

At six on the dot I ring the bell. Mr. St. Claire, who I've never met, opens the door. He's wearing a black suit and silver tie. He looks very dashing.

"Rory, I presume?"

I nod. He steps aside and motions me in. Their house is much bigger and more modern than ours, and very, very clean. Definitely no toddlers living here. It doesn't even look like a ten-year-old lives here. Remembering the opening line Rosemary taught us for a new job, I say, "Thank you for hiring me. I'm very happy to be here with Emily tonight."

He tilts his head in confusion. "Hiring you? Your mom said since this was your first time babysitting, you were doing it on a volunteer basis, for practice."

My mind instantly fills with all the ways I'm going to get Mom back for this.

Mr. St. Claire laughs. "I'm just kidding. You should see your face."

I force a smile. "Good one."

"Come meet Emily," he says, leading us from the entry-way down the hall. As we walk, I pull out the Family Information Form for them to fill out. After a few twists and turns, we wind up in a spotless kitchen where Mrs. St. Claire and Emily are seated at the table, working on home-work. I recognize Mrs. St. Claire now. Tonight she's wearing a shiny purple dress and tall black heels. I don't think I've ever seen people this dressed up for a night out in Willow Falls. I'm already planning on how to describe the dress to Annabelle, who's interested in such things, when I remember that Rosemary said it's an unspoken rule that you don't gossip about the people you sit for because word always gets back.

I say hello to Mrs. St. Claire. She introduces me to Emily, who nods at me pleasantly enough and returns to her homework, her long ponytail swinging around in a graceful arc.

I hand over the form, and then wonder if I should have brought along my Red Cross Babysitting Certificate.

"What's this?" Mrs. St. Claire asks, flipping through the three pages.

Startled at the question, I reply, "It's the Family Information Form."

She leafs through it and laughs. "I don't think even *I* know this much about my family!" She tosses it on the counter and says, "All you need to know are the numbers on the fridge — the doctor, the police, and our cells. Emily's already eaten but help yourself to anything in the kitchen. Bedtime is at eight-forty-five. We'll be home by eleven o'clock. No wild parties."

She and her husband laugh at that last one. They have a strange sense of humor, these two.

"You girls have fun," Mrs. St. Claire says, bending over to kiss the top of Emily's head. "No TV until your homework's done." Turning to me she says, "Call me if anything comes up."

"Okay," I promise. They breeze out of the room, their heels clicking on the floor. I hurry along behind them.

Halfway down the hall, Mr. St. Claire turns around. "Is there a problem, Rory?"

I shake my head. "I'm just, you know, following you to the door."

"Why's that exactly?"

I shift my weight uncomfortably. "You know, to, um, lock the door behind you?"

He starts to laugh, but then Mrs. St. Claire elbows him and he stops. "You know what, Rory," she says, "you're right. That's a much better idea than us locking it from the outside. This way you know it's secure. Maybe we should send all our babysitters to that class."

She pats me on the arm, and I close the door behind them and turn the lock. I'm not sure if she was being sincere or not, but I'm not ready to abandon Rosemary's teachings yet. And just to prove it, I double-check the door and neighboring window, watch that the smoke detector above the front door is blinking to indicate a charged battery, and sniff the air to make sure I don't sense any poisonous gases. Now

I just have to worry about the other eight or nine ways Emily could die tonight under my watch.

When I get back to the kitchen, she's just leaning on her arm, staring down at a math problem, red-faced.

"Everything okay?" I ask, sitting in the chair next to her.

She mumbles that she can't figure out the last math problem.

"I'm pretty good at the basic stuff," I tell her. "Can I take a look?"

"Sure," she says, sliding her math book toward me.

I expect basic fourth grade math. Long division, that sort of thing. What I don't expect to see are tables and graphs with signs and figures that I don't even recognize. I actually turn the book around to make sure it's not upside down. "Um, what is this?"

"I'm kind of in an advanced math class," she explains with a shrug.

"I didn't know we had an advanced math class."

"I go to a private school. In River Bend."

"Oh." I slide the book back to her. "Sorry, I can't help you."

"It's okay," she says, closing it. "If I'm stuck, nobody else in my class will get it, either."

I watch her as she systematically places all her assignments in color-coded folders. Mom hadn't mentioned that this kid was some kind of genius. We learned in class today to try to make the child feel comfortable with you if it's your first time sitting for them. Sure, but who's going to make *me* feel comfortable?

I hear Annabelle's voice in my head. *Man up.* Okay. I take a deep breath. "So do you like school?" Great question, Rory! What kid doesn't hate talking about school? I'm trying to come up with something better when Emily starts talking. She actually talks for a good ten minutes on all the great things about her school. The small class size. The high-tech computer lab. The homemade food in the dining hall, which is what they call their cafeteria. The way it's not too cliquey and everyone respects one another's differences. She says it just like that — *respects one another's differences.*

When she finally runs out of steam, I say, "Wow, that sounds great." I honestly mean it, too.

"Yeah," she acknowledges, "but Jake Harrison is going to be at YOUR school!" She sounds so awestruck that I have to laugh. She laughs, too.

"It's pretty cool, isn't it?" I say.

She nods, wide-eyed. "Have you met him?"

I shake my head. "He's not coming till next week. We're supposed to stay far away from the cast and crew."

"Still, you're going to try, right?"

"For sure!"

We smile at each other. And then a lull creeps into the conversation. She stacks up her books. I drum my fingers in my lap and peek at the clock over the sink. 6:45. That leaves me two hours to fill before Emily's bedtime. Fortunately good old Rosemary has prepared me on how to entertain the older child. I reach for my backpack and pull out a bag of nail polish (compliments of Mom), a pile of comics (compliments of Dad), and a deck of cards (compliments of American Airlines from when we flew to Florida to visit Dad's parents last year). I spread them all out on the table in front of us.

I point to the bag. "A friend of mine likes to paint each of her nails a different color. Wanna try?"

She looks with mild interest at the bag of assorted colors, but shakes her head. "No, thanks."

"Okay, do you like comics?" I spread out the pile a little. "My dad collects first editions."

She leans in to look at them. "And he lets you play with them? I mean, read them?"

I nod. "He doesn't believe in keeping things all sealed up."

"Mine does," she says. "Wanna see something cool?"

"Okay," I say, happy to have something to pass the time.

"C'mon." She jumps up, and I follow her down the hall and up the long staircase to the second floor. We pass many doors, one of which I assume is her bedroom, until we reach a room marked KEEP OUT. She reaches for the knob. A bell goes off in my head, thanks to Rosemary. *Never go into any other rooms in the house other than common rooms. Never invade privacy.*

"Um," I say, putting out my hand. "I don't think we should. I mean, it says 'Keep Out.'"

"It's okay," she assures me. "We won't touch anything."

Before I know it, she's pushed open the door and flicked on the light. My eyes widen. Shelves cover the walls from floor to ceiling. And on the shelves? Hundreds (thousands?) of toys, boxes of candy, comic books, games, and sporting equipment. Everything is in what looks like its original packaging, untouched by human hands.

"Wow!" I say, when I can get out a word. "What *is* all this stuff?"

"My dad's hobby is collecting things and reselling them."

I can't stop staring. My dad's little comic collection looks pretty shabby right about now, and I'm kind of embarrassed. She must have sensed what I was thinking, because she says, "Imagine having all this stuff down the hall from you and not being able to play with it, read it, eat it, or even look at it." She gestures over her shoulder at the KEEP OUT sign.

"That must be hard."

She nods, and I realize she's lonely in this big house that doesn't really feel like a home. It hits me that this babysitting thing is more than just watching someone's kids while they go out. Being in someone's house is like living inside their life for a few hours.

"C'mon," I say, switching off the light. "Let's go back downstairs. We can do anything you want."

Anything she wants turns out to be to watch *High School Musical* on the sixty-inch TV in the living room. So we settle in on the couch, and she puts in the DVD. I wonder if it would be rude to read the book I brought with me for later. I decide it would be, darn it.

They sing, they dance, they sing and dance some more. Emily gets up and dances along to some of them, which is really cute. She seems really free when she dances. "Do you take classes?" I ask her. "You're really good."

"Oh, no," she says, laughing. "You have to be skinny to be a dancer."

"But you're skinny," I point out. "You could totally be a dancer."

She just shakes her head and pinches the side of her belly. She's *ten* and pinching the side of her belly. *I've* never even done that!

The movie's about half over when she asks if I wouldn't mind making some microwave popcorn. She gets a glass bowl out of the cabinet and hands me a packet of fat-free, butter-free (and taste-free) popcorn. I tell her to keep watching the movie without me. So she goes back as I wait the two minutes for it to pop. I can't help noticing there's not a crumb on the counters, no sign of what she ate for dinner.

I bring the bowl of hot popcorn back to the family room and place it on the table in front of us. She nibbles a few pieces while the movie continues, and I start getting twitchy. Finally it ends. I'm about to suggest we play cards, when she says, "Ready for part two?" with such hopefulness that I nod weakly and say, "You bet."

The singing and dancing persist. This time at the country club. Emily happily sings along. I have to fight to stay awake. Emily points me to the bathroom off the hallway. As the credits roll it hits me that it MUST be her bedtime, if not past it! I crane my neck around to look for a clock, and find one over the mantel. 8:20. It's only 8:20?

I turn back to Emily, who is now fumbling with the DVD player. "I thought it must be later," I say, rubbing my eyes.

"They're pretty short movies," she replies, coming back to join me on the couch. "You know, made for TV and all."

"Why don't we go up and get you ready for bed," I say, stretching. Rosemary warned us to start the bedtime routine early, because older kids are likely to stall.

"Just a few more minutes?" she asks as she turns back to the TV. To my horror, *High School Musical 3* begins!

I groan and sink back into the couch. This time they're seniors, and I'm wondering if there's a way to bring back that temporary blindness. The next thing I know, Emily's shaking me. "My parents are home!"

"What, already?" Had I fallen asleep? I jump up and check the clock. 8:30. HUH? How could only ten minutes have passed since the last time I looked? I stare at the clock, then at her, then at the clock again. Events from the night run through my head. Popcorn making. Bathroom breaks. Each time I left the room, she had been turning the clock back! I know I left class a little early, but I'm pretty sure this topic wasn't covered!

"I'm sorry," she whispers. "I won't tell if you don't." And with that, she takes off up the stairs.

That little sneak! Had she been playing me all along? And to think I felt sorry for her. I'm pretty sure falling asleep on the job is frowned upon, so she's got me cornered.

The credits start to roll as the key clicks in the front door. I have just enough time to switch off the TV and try to look awake before the St. Claires come in, laughing and looking as perfect as when they left.

"How did it go?" Mrs. St. Claire asks, shrugging off her long coat.

"Great," I reply, still kind of disoriented. I hope they don't notice. *Please don't ask me if Emily went to bed on time. Please don't ask me if Emily went to bed on time. Please don't ask me if Emily went to bed on time.*

"Did Emily give you any trouble?" Mr. St. Claire asks, pulling out his wallet.

I shake my head, maybe a little too fast.

"I hope we'll see you again," Mrs. St. Claire says. "Roger will drive you home."

I get my bag from the kitchen and stuff my supplies back inside. Sure enough, the clock over the sink says 11:00.

Mom is waiting for me when I get home. "So, how was it?"

"It was . . . educational."

"Are you going to do it again?"

I hold up the handful of five dollar bills. "Definitely!"

But maybe a daytime gig would be better.

Chapter Nine

Because of the babysitting class, my trip to the mall with Annabelle had been moved to Sunday. I'm reminded of this fact by Annabelle shaking me awake and yelling, "Get up! Get up! It's already ten o'clock! The mall opens in half an hour! My mom's waiting downstairs to take us!"

I groan. Why is everyone always waking me up? It feels like two seconds ago that I went to sleep. I roll over and she pulls my pillow out from under me in response.

"Mean!" I yell.

"C'mon, you know I don't like it when our moms hang out for too long."

"All right," I grumble, forcing myself to climb out of the warm, comfy bed. I can't blame her about the mom thing. Her mom always gets temporarily stricter after visiting my house. As I get dressed I tell her about Emily and the clock last night.

"Wow, smart kid! You'll have to make sure Rosemary adds that one to the handbook."

She follows me into the bathroom, telling me about the plan she and Sari came up with last night to get into Jake's trailer. I have to push her out and close the door. "A little privacy, please." She leans against the door and keeps talking.

In the kitchen, our moms are drinking coffee. They stop talking when they see us, which is annoying. But I guess we'd do the same thing if they came in on one of our conversations.

Mom hands me an English muffin and the lecture begins. "Don't talk to strangers. Don't spend all your money. Don't fill up on junk food in the food court. Keep your phone on and within reach."

She follows us out to the car, her slippers flapping on the driveway. Annabelle's mom holds the back door open for me and I scurry inside. Mom leans into the open window. "And don't come home with a bunny!"

"Wow, those are a lot of rules," Annabelle says, turning around in her seat.

"And all very sensible," her mother adds, glancing pointedly at Annabelle. "You'd do well to follow them, too."

Annabelle shoots me a look, which I pretend not to see.

The mall seems bigger than when I was here with Dad. Annabelle and I stand just inside the doorway, soaking it all in. She's come here with her older brothers for years, but they won't go into any of the stores she likes. Even *I* won't go into some of the stores she likes, like the one where they only sell hair accessories. Sari got Annabelle hooked on it. They can spend hours in there.

"Where should we go first?" I ask.

"I just heard about a new makeup store where all the makeup is natural," she says. "I'm not sure where it is, though."

"Natural?"

"Like made of healthy stuff. You know, natural ingredients."

Before I can ask more, a group of three high school girls walk by, swinging shopping bags and giggling. Annabelle grabs my arm and hurries after them. I would never have the nerve to talk to them, but Annabelle has no fear.

"Do you know where the new makeup store is?" she asks the group. "Where they make you up for free and everything's, like, natural?"

They stop walking. One of them turns to the others and says, "Yeah, we just saw that, right?"

The tallest of the girls taps a long red nail against her

chin like she's trying to think, and says, "Right, now where was it?"

"I know!" the third one says. "It was upstairs, near Macy's. You should take that elevator over there." She points down one of the alleys nearby. "That's a shortcut."

"Thanks!" Annabelle gushes, and then adds, "I like your nails."

But they just giggle and keep walking. As we head to the elevator, I ask, "We're not going to be like that when we're in high school, are we?"

"Like what?" Annabelle asks.

When we reach the elevator it has just opened, even though no one else is waiting there, and no one gets out. "Never mind," I say. "Let's just get on."

We run in just before the doors close. I notice right away that it doesn't look like an ordinary elevator. For one thing, it is much smaller and narrower and the walls are covered in some foamy kind of material. It makes me want to touch it.

"Um," Annabelle says, pointing to the walls. "Do you see any buttons to press?"

I don't. I don't see any buttons at all, even the ones above the door that tell you what floor you're on. "Okay, this is really weird."

Annabelle tries pushing on the doors. Nothing happens. She tries wedging her fingers between them and pulling. Nothing. "Are we even moving?" she asks.

"I don't think so, but it's hard to tell." My palms start to sweat and I wipe them on my pants. "Is it getting hot in here?"

"Well!" exclaims Annabelle. "This is a fine kettle of fish!"

I laugh and think of my grandmother, and that makes me feel better.

Annabelle starts pounding on the doors. "Hello! Anyone? We're stuck in here!"

Suddenly I remember my phone and pull it out. No signal. Figures. The one time I really need it.

We pound for a few more minutes, and without warning, the doors begin to open with a clanking noise. We jump back. A burly man in overalls leans on a big stack of boxes, arms crossed in front of him. "What are you two doing in there?"

We hurry out, careful to keep out of his way. "Um, we were just trying to get upstairs," Annabelle says.

He points to the sign on the wall. A sign we hadn't noticed before. FREIGHT ONLY. NO PASSENGERS.

"Oh," I say, backing up farther. "Sorry, didn't see that."

"You're lucky I came along," he grumbles, pushing the boxes inside, then stepping back out and pushing the button. The doors close, and this time I can clearly hear the elevator rising, clanking as it goes.

"Um, so where did those boxes just go?" Annabelle asks.

The guy looks at us like we must be the two stupidest girls on the planet. "They go upstairs. Someone else takes 'em out."

"Oh," we say, nodding and backing up even farther. "Well, thanks!" He just shakes his head as we run back to the main part of the mall. We don't stop running until we're far out of sight and then start laughing.

"Let's agree to never tell anyone what just happened," I say.

"Agreed," Annabelle says. But then she adds, "Maybe we should tell those girls, though, so they don't get stuck, too."

That's Annabelle. Always thinking the best of people.

"We'll tell them if we run into them again," I promise, very much hoping we don't. I look around to get my bearings. We happen to be near the pet store. "C'mon, I want to show you my bunny."

Annabelle follows me inside and instantly covers her nose. "Ew, what's that smell?"

I gaze at Kyle adoringly. "That's the smell of love."

"I sure hope not," she says, bending down next to me. "So this is the guy?"

I nod. "I was worried he wouldn't still be here."

"He's really, really cute," Annabelle says, sticking in a finger to pet his nose. "Is your mom ever gonna let you get him?"

"If I can prove I have enough money to take care of him." I pat the wad of cash in my front pocket. "I almost have enough now."

"Hey, you're gonna need that money to get ready for the audition. No offense, but we really need to stand out. And one of us needs a little more work in that area."

"I know. I wasn't planning on getting him today. You heard my mom."

The manager is behind the counter and I ask him if anyone had shown any interest in him over the week.

"Actually, yeah," he says. "He got sold."

I gasp and clutch Annabelle's arm.

"But they returned him. As you can see."

I relax my grip and Annabelle squirms away. "Why?" I ask.

"Didn't give me the details," he says with a shrug, and continues stacking cat food cans behind the counter.

Annabelle points to her watch. "Let's go. We have a lot to do."

As we head out of the store, I say to Annabelle, "Kyle knew he wouldn't be happy with some other family, that's why they had to return him. They knew he was meant to be with me."

"Uh-huh," Annabelle says. "Some little kid was probably allergic."

I like my theory better.

"You're going to change his name, right?"

I nod. "What do you think about . . . Bunny?"

"You're going to name your bunny, Bunny?"

"Sure, why not?"

As we pass the store with the ear piercing station, Annabelle suddenly stops. "How cool would you look at the audition wearing those earrings your grandmother gave you?"

"My mom already said she'd bring me next week."

"Yeah, but that'll be too late. We're here now and the audition's tomorrow."

"But I don't have them with me."

"That's okay," she says, pushing me into the store. "You have to get them pierced with special pointy ones anyway."

She tells the lady behind the counter that I want my ears pierced. The woman (who has earrings in at least ten body parts that I can see) points out the ones I get to choose from for the initial piercing. She calls them "starter" earrings, and there aren't too many options. The standard gold balls that I've seen in many classmates' ears over the years, some fake diamond ones, and that's pretty much it. I pick out the balls, and we go stand behind a preppy teenage boy, the only other person on line.

"I can't believe I'm finally going to do this!"

"It'll look great."

"Does it hurt?"

"Nah."

"How would you know, you were three months old!"

"Everyone wouldn't do it if it hurt so much, right?"

"I guess that's true."

The piercing lady tells the boy to sit down on the stool while she grabs a cotton ball. He looks a little pale to me, with a line of sweat on his upper lip. She dips the cotton into a container marked ANTISEPTIC, and then wipes the first ear. He squirms a little and I feel like I'm invading his privacy by watching, so I turn away and admire a row of pretty earrings that I'll actually be able to wear soon.

Then the screaming begins. "Ow! It hurts!" I whirl around. The boy is clutching at his ear. "The blood," he yells, "the blood!"

The lady stands next to him, helpless. I see what looks like a gun in her hand. "But I didn't even do it yet," she protests. "I just drew the dot so I'd know where to pierce."

But the boy is not falling for that old trick and I don't blame him. I stash the gold balls on the nearest shelf and grab Annabelle. "We're going."

She stumbles along behind me, trying to argue me back into the store. "That kid was just a wimp. You'll be fine!"

"I'll do it with my mom," I promise when I get her out of the store. "If you let it drop, I'll go with you to the hair accessories place."

"Really?" Annabelle says. "Okay!"

But when we get there it just looks so boring, all those barrettes and bows and bands and extensions. I stare longingly at the bookstore next door. She sighs. "Go. I'll meet you there."

"Thanks!" I run out and straight through the bookstore into the children's section. I love coming here and picking out a book. I always feel like whatever I find is exactly what I need to find at that moment. A woman who looks a few years older than my mom is browsing in the children's section, too. We exchange small smiles as I kneel down a few feet away. She has two books on her lap, trying to decide between them. I can't help looking.

"I really loved that one," I say to her, pointing to the closest one. The other I don't recognize.

"Really?" she says. "Then you should read this one. It's the sequel."

My eyes widen. "No way!" I practically grab it out of her hand. "I didn't know there was a sequel! Thank you!"

She smiles as I clutch the book to my chest. Just then the store manager comes by and the woman gets up to follow him. I bring my book up to the front to pay for it, and hear them talking.

"I'm sorry," he says, "but I can't hire you without previous bookstore experience."

The woman frowns, and I can see now how tired she looks.

Looking down at the book in my hand, and then back up, I say loudly, "Hey, thanks again for all your help. I never would have found this without you."

The woman turns around, surprised. I keep gushing. "I mean, you knew just what I wanted and where to find it and I was about to give up and leave." Turning to the manager I say, "You should give this lady a raise."

"I don't actually work here," she says, flustered.

The manager clears his throat and slides an application form across the counter to her. "Why don't you just fill this out and we'll see what we can do." He turns around to grab a pen and she smiles at me gratefully.

By the time I'm done paying, Annabelle still hasn't surfaced from the hair store. I text her from the bookstore and remind her we only have an hour left before her mom is coming to pick us up. Within two minutes she appears in front of me, a hot-pink stripe down the left side of her head.

"Whoa! Are you trying to be like my dad?"

"Yes, I've always idolized your dad and want to be more like him."

"Okay, I know it's weird that my dad has a blue stripe in his hair, but he gets *paid* for wearing his."

"I will, too," she says triumphantly. "When I get picked to be in the movie!" She points to my bag. "You didn't spend all your money on a book did you? You'll need it for the makeup."

"It's just a paperback," I tell her. "It probably cost less than the stripe."

She grins. "Probably. C'mon, I found out where the makeup store is. I hope it's not too crowded."

It's actually totally empty when we arrive. Two women are straightening some jars behind the counter. "Makeovers?" the younger one says hopefully.

"For her," Annabelle says, pointing at me. The women

spring into action. They rush me onto a tall stool and turn my face left and right. Makes me wish I washed my face this morning.

"I'm Debbie," the younger one says, "and this is Sue."

"I'm Rory."

"That's a pretty name," Debbie says.

I throw a look at Annabelle as if to say, *See? I don't always get the boy comment.*

"I have a nephew named Rory," Sue says.

Annabelle stifles a laugh. I just sigh.

"So what are you looking for today, Rory?" Debbie asks.

Before I can answer, Annabelle says, "She's allowed to wear makeup now, and we have a big audition to go to tomorrow. And a party soon. So she needs to look good."

"You've come to the right place. Young skin like yours doesn't need all those harsh chemicals and preservatives like other makeup lines have. Everything here comes from plants and natural extracts." She pauses, waiting for my response.

"Sounds good," I say eagerly.

"Great," Debbie says. "Let's get started."

The makeover begins with a frenzy of activity. Debbie whisks off my glasses and hands them to me. I pass them to Annabelle. Bottles and jars and pencils are uncapped, powders are opened, and lipsticks are twisted. Sponges and wedges are laid out along with brushes of all sizes. "This will even out the blotchiness," Sue says, applying something silky all over my face.

"And this will brighten up your sallow complexion," Debbie says, sponging on something from a pink bottle. I don't know what sallow means, but it doesn't sound like a compliment.

Sue paints something from a brown jar down the sides of my nose. "This will make your nose look smaller," she explains. Is my nose big? Do I have some huge honking nose and don't know it?

She tells me to look up as she strokes eyeliner in the outer corners of my eyes. It's hard not to flinch when someone comes toward your eye with something resembling a stick. "This will make your eyes look not so close together," she says. Then switching to a different pencil for my lips, she adds, "and your lips not so thin."

Why didn't anyone tell me I was so hideous? Thank God I'm getting the help I need now.

"And we're done!" Debbie declares after applying one more dab of gloss to my lower lip. "Want to see?"

I nod eagerly. She spins me around to face the mirror. I gasp. "Is that me?" I stand up to look closer. I'd see better with my glasses on, but don't want to cover up all the hard work they did on my eyes.

"Wow!" Annabelle says. "You look amazing!"

I do! I look amazing! Somehow they got rid of my baby fat. I have cheekbones! I stare into the mirror, trying to burn this image of myself into my brain.

"You look older," Annabelle says, nodding appreciatively.

I reach for my money. "How much is it?"

The women smile, and begin totaling up the bill. Annabelle pulls me aside.

"You don't need to buy *everything*," she whispers. "Some things you can get at the drugstore for much cheaper."

"But not all-natural like these," I point out.

"Still. Think of the bunny."

I can't help but admire myself in the mirror again. "Think of Jake Harrison!" I reply.

"Bunny!"

"Jake!"

"BUNNY!"

Debbie clears her throat and hands me a slip of paper. I look down at it. The total cost is more than all my babysitting money, plus birthday and Christmas! And there is that little matter of the bunny. I sigh. "Okay, how much for whatever took away the blotchiness?"

"Twelve dollars."

"I'll take it."

As I'm digging through my pockets for the cash, Annabelle says, "Um, Debbie? Is that normal?"

I look up to see Annabelle staring at the right side of my face. Debbie and Sue lean in for a better look.

"Hmm," Sue murmurs. "Haven't seen that happen before."

"Why? What is it?" I turn around and look in the mirror. The right side of my face is round again. Not a cheekbone in sight. "Did the makeup wear off on that side already?"

"Just a sec," Debbie tells us. She waves Sue over to a desk in the corner of the store. They bend their heads together and start searching the drawers for something.

"Um," Annabelle says, "does your eye, uh, hurt at all?"

"My eye? No." But as I say it, it does sort of tingle a little. I peer in the mirror. It's a bit puffy and red. My right cheek is definitely getting bigger, though. That's weird.

Sue comes back over to us. "You may be having a reaction to one of the ingredients in the makeup."

"But what about the all-natural thing?" Annabelle asks. "Isn't this makeup supposed to be really healthy?"

"This almost never happens," Sue swears.

My other eye is starting to water.

A customer walks in the store and starts looking at the displays of lipstick. "Can you come back a little later?" Sue asks, guiding the woman gently out of the store. "We're just finishing up with this client." It might be my imagination, but it almost seemed like Sue positioned herself between me and the customer.

"Here it is," Debbie says, pulling a crumpled sheet of paper from behind the desk and uncreasing it. "Okay. It says the first thing to do is to get all the makeup off. That should help things considerably." They lead me to a sink in the back of the shop. Along the way I catch my reflection. Both eyes are red and puffy now, like I haven't slept in a few days. My left cheek is quite large, too. Otherwise it's not *that* bad. I still think I look pretty amazing.

They give me some soap and a towel, and it just feels like such a waste to wash off this incredible makeup job. "You should hurry," Sue urges. I close my eyes, recalling the vision in the mirror of only a few minutes ago, when I looked perfect. Reluctantly, I begin to wash it off, revealing my thin lips, huge nose, and sallow complexion.

When I'm done drying my face, I lower the towel and ask, "All better?"

No one answers. Debbie hurries back to the desk to consult the paper. I turn back toward the mirror, but Annabelle grabs me first and says, "We better go."

I'm not in any big hurry to see the Old Me anyway; it would just be depressing. I'd rather imagine I still have all the makeup on. "All right, let me just pay for the anti-blotch stuff."

Sue waves off my money. "I think you probably want to stay away from all plant-based products for a while."

"Oh." I rub my eye. "Okay."

"And try to avoid rubbing," she adds.

I turn to Annabelle and ask for my glasses back. When I try to put them on, they pop back into my hand, like they're suddenly too small for my face. Annabelle sees me fumbling and takes them.

"Let's hold off on those for a little bit," she suggests, "till the swelling goes down."

On our way out of the store, Debbie slips Annabelle the instructions. They exchange a few words, and I hear Annabelle promise to call them with an update, which, honestly, feels a little unnecessary.

"Where should we go now?" I ask.

Annabelle stares at me. "Don't you want to go home?"

"Why? We still have some time."

"Um, well, your face is a little swollen."

That's what *she* might see, but not what I see. I see shiny pink lips, smooth unblotchy skin, sculpted cheekbones, and sparkly eyes. "I'm fine," I insist. "Let's just keep walking around."

"Well, if you say so," she says uneasily. Every few feet I have to apologize for bumping into her. It's a bit hard to see straight without my glasses. I narrowly avoid bumping into a sunglasses kiosk.

"Your friend okay?" the guy manning the booth asks.

"She's fine," Annabelle snaps, holding on to my arm. "Hey, I owe you a birthday present. How about a pair of sunglasses?"

"Sure!" I say, squinting to see them clearly. "You might need to pick them out, though."

"Try these." She slips a pair onto my face. It's like someone dimmed the lights. I feel around the edges with my hands.

"They feel kind of big. You don't think they cover too much of my face?"

"No, they're perfect," she insists. "How much?"

"Five dollars," the guy says. "Is she contagious? Because —"

Annabelle cuts him off. "She's *fine.*"

It's getting harder to keep the image of Beautiful Rory in my head with this kind of talk flying around me. The cool shades help, though. Now I'm Glamorous Hollywood Rory, shielding my eyes from my adoring fans. But I can barely see anything, so I push them up on top of my head. Annabelle pulls them back down again.

"I think you should keep them on."

"But I can't see!"

"That's okay. It's worth it because you look so cool."

I shrug. Annabelle knows much more about cool than I do. I stick close to her as we make our way back to the other end of the mall where we'll be getting picked up.

"Omigod!" she exclaims. "The film crew is eating at the food court!"

"So?"

"So we're not allowed to talk to them at school, but the principal didn't say anything about what happens *off* school property. C'mon." She drags me with her until the smell of Panda Pavilion mixed with Nathan's Hot Dogs and Cinnabon nearly overwhelms me. They stop talking when we approach.

"Hi," Annabelle gushes, "we're trying out to be extras and wondered, um, like, is there anything we should or shouldn't do that would help us get picked?" Even with my limited sight, I can tell she's running her hand through the section of her hair with the stripe.

"Honestly, girls," one of the women says, "the best thing to do is not to stand out in any way."

"What do you mean?" Annabelle asks, clearly not expecting this answer.

"Look at it like this," the woman begins. "The director doesn't want anyone in the background of the scene to detract from the main action, right? So he's going to be looking for people who blend in. People who he can use in different settings without the viewer recognizing them."

"Oh," Annabelle says in a small voice. I don't blame her for being disappointed. She's not someone who easily blends in. Even without the stripe, her blond hair has an inner glow that can be seen clear across the school yard. And her colorful wardrobe doesn't help, either.

One of the guys asks, "Hey, is it sunny in here?" It takes a minute for me to realize he's teasing me about my sunglasses. I slip them off and he literally jumps back in his chair and says to Annabelle, "Whoa, what happened to your friend?"

"You should see the other guy!" Annabelle quips, and they all laugh. "Put them back on," she hisses in my ear. I rub my itchy eyes, scratch my cheek, and do as she says.

"Is it really that bad?" I ask when we're far enough away.

"It's getting worse," she says. "You kinda look like a boxer who lost his match. I'm gonna call my mom and tell her we're ready to go."

When Mrs. Richardson sees me, she says, "I'll be right back," and then walks a few feet away to use her phone. I can tell from her end of the conversation that she's speaking to my mother. "Tell her I didn't get the bunny!" I call out.

"Or fill up on junk food!" Annabelle adds.

Dad opens the door when I get home, which is a good thing because it would have been hard to find the keyhole with my key. He makes an odd little noise in his throat when he sees me, then quickly covers it up by saying, "Hey, you don't look so bad."

"Really?" I ask. I think my lips might be a little swollen because the word comes out sounding more like, "Ree-ey?"

He nods. "Really."

I take off my sunglasses. He flinches, but keeps his smile steady.

Then Sawyer comes into the hall, dragging a wagon full of LEGOs. He takes one look at me and screams with all his strength, which is considerable. He drops the wagon and cowers in the corner, hands over his face, shrieking.

"Um, he saw a spider," Dad says. "That wasn't about you or anything."

Mom rushes in to see what's going on. Then she turns right back around and calls the doctor at home. Two teaspoonfuls of allergy medicine later, I'm lying on the couch with a mixture of baking soda and oatmeal slathered on my face.

Sawyer runs into the room, shrieks again, and runs out.

Without opening my mouth too far, I ask Dad, "Another spider?"

"No. This time it was you."

Chapter Ten

I put down my glass of orange juice when Mom comes into the kitchen. "On a scale of one to ten, how bad is it?"

"Tilt your head to the left."

I comply.

She sizes me up. "Is ten good, or is ten bad?"

"Never mind." I make a mental note to find out if ten is actually good or bad.

"You can barely tell," Dad assures me, coming up from behind and kissing me on top of my head. "The medicine is definitely working."

I glance over at Sawyer, who is climbing into his chair. He starts to whimper and looks away.

"Sawyer won't even look at me."

"At least he's not screaming anymore," Dad points out, grabbing a piece of toast.

"I guess." I check the clock. It's time for another spoonful of medicine. Mom had come in every four hours last night to dose me up. I grab my book bag from the floor and stick on my new sunglasses. Once they're on, I feel more secure. Dad loosened the screws on my regular glasses so they fit again. The sunglasses are so big they fit right over my regular ones.

"Do you want me to drive you?" Mom asks.

"That's okay. Remember the auditions are today, so I'll be home late."

"Break a leg," Dad says, holding the door open for me.

"Now why would you say a thing like that?" I hear Mom scold Dad as I hurry outside.

I've started to enjoy the solitary walk to school. One time last week I tried reading while I walked, but fell off the curb and almost twisted my ankle. Now I just go over things in my head, like the fact that I didn't get any homework done over the weekend. And that Jake Harrison is going to be in school today. Darn my sensitive skin!

As I climb the stairs up to the school, a girl calls my name. I stop and look around. The voice is coming from a tall, brown-haired girl in a plain brown T-shirt, jeans, and Keds. She looks sort of familiar. I take off my sunglasses. "Annabelle? Is that you?"

"It's me!" she says, throwing back her shoulders.

"Wow! You look totally different!"

Annabelle whirls around so I can see all sides of her. "Average? Blend-in-able?"

I nod. "Definitely!"

"Thanks! My mom totally freaked when she saw my hair. But it'll rinse out in a few weeks. Your face looks really good. You almost can't tell."

I let the *almost* slide. As we walk to our lockers, I can't help but notice that nearly all the girls in the school are dressed up today. Makeup, hair down, skirts even! I also can't help noticing how a lot of them have shaved their legs. It makes me wish I'd bumped that up on my list. Annabelle says she tried to sneak over to the trailers, but security had been stepped up and she couldn't get close.

"Do you think he's really here?" I ask. "Like, breathing the same air we are?"

She nods. "I can feel it, can't you?"

I nod.

After being admonished in my first two classes for not having my homework, I ask for a bathroom pass to check my face. My mom had packed me some medicine to take if

I needed it, but I don't want to get groggy and fall asleep in class. That wouldn't go over too well. The lighting in the bathroom leaves a lot to be desired. It doesn't hide any flaws. Sallow skin is on full display. To someone who didn't know me, I might almost look normal. To everyone else, though, I'm still a little swollen. Not like a boxer anymore, but not like regular Rory, either. I'm about to enter one of the stalls when I hear a girl's voice out in the hallway.

"I can go to the bathroom by myself! I'm not five years old!"

I hurry into the stall so I don't have to deal with whoever it is. I twist the lock just as the bathroom door bangs open (which isn't easy to do because it's one of those heavy doors). Whoever it is must be wearing heels because I can hear them click-clacking on the floor. I peek through the slat in the stall door and almost fall back into the toilet. It's Madison Waters! In *my* school bathroom! She's even more beautiful in person, which is annoying. Shiny black hair, perfect Hollywood tan, brown lace-up sandals with tall heels, and a skirt way too short to pass the school's dress code. I try not to breathe as she starts punching numbers into her cell phone.

"It's me," Madison says. "I'm here in Podunk, U.S.A."

I want to correct her and say, *Actually, it's Willow Falls,* but restrain myself.

"Yeah, he's here, too. We just had breakfast in my trailer. Woulda been more fun if the stupid PA wasn't there, too. They don't leave us alone together for a minute."

My heart pounds harder. She's talking about Jake! He *is* here!

"What? No way." She laughs. "The ring is just for publicity. Yeah, he's totally gorgy, but he wants to be an *actor*."

She says *actor* like it's a bad word.

"Me? I want to be a movie star, and he's just gonna drag me down. He wants to do *plays*!" She laughs again. The bathroom door swings open, and someone else comes in. "I better go," she says hurriedly. Then there's some kind of crash and things go skittering across the floor. I peek out again.

"Watch it," Madison says, rescuing her cell phone from under the row of sinks.

"I'm so sorry!" a girl's voice says, breathless. I can't see her from this angle.

"What's this?" Madison asks, pointing to a book that had fallen open on the floor. "Hey! Is that my boyfriend in your photo album?"

"It's nothing," the girl insists, an edge of panic in her voice. I gasp as I realize it must be Kira, the girl from the babysitting class. Without thinking, I fumble to flush the toilet and leave the stall as nonchalantly as possible.

Madison turns and stares at me with instant suspicion. Kira's eyes are pleading.

I stroll right up to where the book is lying on the floor, and before Madison can reach for it again, I bend down and grab it. I close it quickly and give it to Kira, who clutches it tight and runs out of the bathroom.

"That girl is always dropping things," I say, turning on the faucet to wash my hands. My heart is pounding out of my chest. I can see Madison staring at me in the mirror, but I pretend not to notice. "Have a great day," I say, breezing out of the bathroom. Good thing my chair is attached to my desk, because I almost collapse when I get back to class. I don't hear a single thing my bio teacher says all period.

At lunch, Annabelle and Sari make me tell and retell the story five times to make sure I haven't left out a single detail.

"Was she wearing the ring?" Sari asks.

"I didn't look. I was too busy trying not to pass out."

"I wonder what a PA is," she says. "Personal Assistant maybe?"

"Do you think she knows you heard everything?" Annabelle asks, wide-eyed.

"Probably." For once, I think my inability to stand out will work in my favor. "Hopefully she won't recognize me if she sees me again."

Natalie Karp, Mena, and Alexa walk by. They're dressed up like they're going to a party. Or at least what I imagine people would wear to a party. Mena and Alexa ignore us as usual, but Natalie stops and points to Annabelle. "What happened to your hair?"

I know Annabelle can't tell them the real reason, or else Natalie would ask why she didn't let *her* in on what the lady at the mall said. "I just wanted a change," she says with a shrug.

Mena and Alexa laugh as the three of them move along. "Good day for it!" Alexa says. "More chance for *us* to get picked at the audition!"

Annabelle just smiles and sips her soda. I can't help thinking that at least they had seen Annabelle as a threat, something they would never think about me.

The auditions are held in the gym. We're told to sit on the bleachers while the crew gets organized. Half the school must be here. The girls are all hoping to see Jake, and the boys are trying to catch a glimpse of Madison. As if either of them would just be hanging out in the gym. The same crew member who gave us the advice at the mall stands up and tells us to quiet down, which we instantly do. She's wearing a headset with a little microphone in front of her mouth.

"Hi, everyone. I'm the AD," she says, smiling. "That means Assistant Director. It's my job to organize the extras. How many of you have been in a movie before?"

We all burst out laughing as if that's the funniest thing we ever heard, and she joins in. "Okay, well, it's nothing to be intimidated by. Actors are real people just like you and me. In fact, to prove it, I'd like to introduce you to a few."

Our heads swivel to the left as the gym door swings open. In walk Jake and Madison, waving and smiling, flanked on both sides by security guards. We all jump to our feet and clap. It's weird to be clapping for someone just because they walked into the room, but that's what we're doing. Annabelle is gripping my arm so hard I think she's going to leave a bruise. On Annabelle's other side, Sari is gripping *hers*. Jake is even more "gorgy" in person, even though he looks a little older than I expected. One of the other crew members hands him a cordless mike. "Thank you, Willow Falls, for welcoming us! I know this is going to be a great movie! I bet you're all wondering what the name of the movie is. . . ."

That statement brings on another round of clapping and whooping.

"Well, we're going to tell you right now, aren't we, Madison?"

Madison makes a big show of nodding her head excitedly. Maybe she's a better actress than I thought. She grabs the microphone and says, *"Playing It Cool!"*

Everyone cheers again, even though it doesn't really tell us anything about what kind of movie it is. Romantic comedy? Musical? Horror? I hope it's not horror. Or musical.

Jake and Madison wave again and are ushered back out of the gym. It all happened so fast I almost think I dreamt it. The red welt on my arm tells me otherwise, though.

The AD steps forward again. "I wish we could work with all of you," she says sincerely, "but contractually we're only allowed to take thirty extras. So, that said, let's get to it. The director will make the selections, and then I'll have to ask the rest of you to leave. Thank you."

A minute later, a short, balding man with a matching headset marches up to the front of the room and barks, "Front row, stand and line up against the wall." The front row doesn't move. I don't blame them. It was just such a surprise after the niceness of the AD.

"Up," he repeats, motioning upward with his arms. Then he points and says, "Wall."

Murmuring and grabbing their bags, the front row scurries to do as he says. Standing against the wall, they look like convicts in a police lineup. Very young and nervous convicts. He walks quickly down the line, his hands clasped behind his back. Some kids look down as his gaze momentarily falls on them, others stare right back. I'm betting that the ones who're looking down will have a better chance of getting chosen, since they're the ones more likely to blend in. But to my surprise, it doesn't happen that way. "You," he says, pointing to a short, dark-haired boy. "You, you, and you." He points to more kids, all of whom had been looking up. And all of whom are really normal looking. He passes right by Alexa and Mena, barely looking at them at all. Mena makes a noise deep in her throat. He stops, glances at her dismissively, and keeps going. Her face falls. I actually feel a pang of sympathy for her. He waves his hand, and the AD hurries over and tells the rest of the kids they can go. The few kids chosen are ushered into the back of the gym to wait.

You could hear a pin drop in the bleachers as the first row files out of the gym, grumbling. This time, when the director tells the second row (my row) to stand up, we spring to our feet and hurry into place. On the way, I whisper to Annabelle and Sari to keep eye contact with him. They nod. Just before the director starts power-walking down the line, the back door of the gym cracks open and my jaw falls as Jake Harrison slips in, no security guard or anything. Just him. Alone. Twenty yards away from us. No one in the crew seems to notice him, and I get the feeling he wants it that way.

My heart starts racing again, and I wonder how much excitement one person can take in a day. I'm glad there's a solid wall behind me in case I faint. Annabelle and I wind up in the middle of the line, and Sari is a few spots farther down. By the time the director gets to us, he's already chosen five kids. It takes all my willpower to meet his eyes, especially with Jake watching, but I do it. He points to me and then to Annabelle, who lets out a squeal of delight. The director stops and glares at her. She leans against the wall and tries to look innocent. Then he glances at me, and backs up until he's facing me full-on. I hold my breath, hoping he's not going to change his mind. He waves his hands around my head. "What's with your face?"

Maybe I shouldn't have worn my glasses. They sort of magnify the swelling. Unable to look anywhere but the floor, I reply, "Allergic reaction. It's almost gone."

"Yeah," Annabelle pipes in. "Yesterday she was, like, an *eight*, and now she's only a two."

I'm hoping a two is better than an eight on her scale of how bad I look. I really should get clarification on that.

"Fine," the director says, waving me off with a flip of his hand. He continues down the row where he chooses six more people. But Sari isn't one of them! Did she not meet his eyes? Should she not have worn the Hello Kitty barrette? To her credit, Sari doesn't give in to her usual dramatic tendencies and collapse and pound her fists on the gym floor. She just gives me and Annabelle an encouraging smile as she follows the others out of the gym. Annabelle whispers, "Don't feel bad. Sari told me she didn't really want to do it anyway."

"Why?"

"Something about stage fright. She barely managed not to lose her lunch before this!"

I never would have guessed that about Sari. It does make me feel better, though.

It might be my imagination, and it probably is, but I swear when I pass by Jake he gives me the thumbs-up. The next time I look, he's gone.

The chosen group grows steadily as each row takes their turn. Amanda, Leo, and his friends Jimmy and Vinnie are chosen, along with Kira and a few others from our grade. Mostly, though, the group is made up of seventh and eighth graders. When everyone has been selected and the other kids have left the gym, the AD comes over and says, "Okay, now the real work begins."

But we're too busy jumping and whooping to hear her. She waits patiently until we settle down. "My name is

Brenda, and here are the rules. We never know when our shooting schedule will require you, so you'll need to be 'on call' at all times. If you miss one scene, you're out. Sorry, but we can't get stuck short at the last minute. You'll need to have changes of clothes ready. Dressy clothes, casual school clothes, gym clothes, pants, shorts, shoes. No advertisements or brand names on the clothes. No busy patterns or bright colors. No looking at the camera when we're rolling, no talking to the actors, no complaining how long it takes to film one scene."

For the next hour, she teaches us how to make believe we're talking without any words actually coming out of our mouths. She calls this "fake talk." This is what we'll be doing in the background of a scene. It's supposed to look real, but won't interfere with what the actors are saying. So we take turns mouthing words silently to one another. Right before dismissing us, one of the PAs (which we've learned means Production Assistant) hands out forms for us to fill in with our names and phone numbers. As we line up to hand them back in, Brenda says, "Be ready on Wednesday for our first scene. It'll be an outdoor soccer game. Shorts, plain-colored T-shirts, sneakers."

I can't help but glance down at my legs. It's not like there's so much hair I could *braid* it or anything, but they're not *movie* legs. Movie legs are long and smooth and shiny.

There's nothing I can do about the long part, but I can do smooth and shiny. I pull Annabelle aside and point down at my legs. She nods knowingly and fake-talks, "Tomorrow after school."

"Sounds good," I fake-talk back. Hair-free legs, here I come. How hard could it be?

Chapter Eleven

At the drugstore, Annabelle knows just where to find the shaving stuff because three of her older brothers shave already. We stare at the rows and rows of products. Razors and lotions and waxes and shaving creams of all shapes and sizes and colors. I glance down at Annabelle's legs. Her wispy blond hair will probably come off in two seconds. *I'm* gonna need the strong stuff. "How are we supposed to choose from all this?"

She starts grabbing random items off the shelves and dropping them into the plastic basket she'd picked up on our way in. "We'll just have to try one of each thing to see what works."

"I have to save my money for the bunny, remember?"

"No problem," she says, whipping a twenty dollar bill out of her pocket.

"Where did you get that?"

"My parents gave it to me as an advance on the money we're going to get paid as extras."

"But how did you know you'd get picked?"

"I knew," she says.

I've always admired Annabelle's confidence. And now, I'm admiring her generosity, even though it turns out our stuff costs almost thirty dollars, so I have to dig into the bunny money after all.

Choosing my house over hers is an easy decision. Foot-shaped hole in bathroom door beats five boys running around, no question. We empty the bags on my bed and have to scramble to catch the cans before they roll off. Annabelle's phone rings. I recognize her mom's ringtone. While she takes the call I busy myself lining up all the boxes and cans in size order.

"Can't you just pick me up later?" she asks. "We're in the middle of something really important. Oh, okay, I'll be right out." She puts her phone back in her pocket. "Sorry, gotta go. My mom's swinging by to pick me up. She's having a dinner party and says I have to be there."

I wave my arm at the bed. "How am I supposed to do this alone?"

She grabs a few items and tosses them back into one of the bags. "I have faith in you."

"But you shouldn't." I follow after her as she sprints down the hall. "You should have very little faith in me."

"Sorry! Bye!" she says, bounding down the stairs. "Text me if you're in trouble."

For a split second, I consider asking Mom to help me. But it's just too awkward and embarrassing. I can't make myself do it. Returning to my room, I pick up what Annabelle left on the bed: shaving cream, two different kinds of razors, and a box of wax that will require the microwave. That will be Plan B. The woman on the shaving cream can looks very confident as she runs the razor up her leg. The shaving cream parts to reveal perfectly smooth, silky skin. It looks easy enough. Even a non-girly girl like me should be able to figure it out. I march into the bathroom, stuff a towel into the hole in the door, and get to work.

Choosing between the razors is easy. I pick the one with only one blade since it looks less intimidating, and wrestle it out of the plastic packaging. Then I pull the cap off the can and shake it up like it's whipped cream. I press the button on the top, and a big dollop of shaving cream squirts out, looking like soft serve ice cream but probably not tasting like it.

I scoop it into my other hand, lift my leg until it's resting on the counter, and spread the shaving cream in a long line from my ankle to my knee. I squirt, scoop, and apply until my leg is completely covered, with no hair showing through anywhere. With a deep breath, I place the razor at my ankle, and slowly draw it upward. All it does is take off a layer of shaving cream. Maybe I piled it on too thick? I wipe some off on a towel until it's about half as thick and I can see the tops of the hair. This is very messy. I have to grip on to the counter to keep from slipping, getting shaving cream from my hands onto the countertop in the process.

Take two, as they say in the movie biz. This time I can see the razor is making contact with my skin. I think it's working! Hair is definitely piling up on the top of the razor as I slide it up! And I don't even feel it! When I get to my knee, I turn the razor over in my hand and start back down. The razor is about halfway to my ankle when the pain registers in my brain. OW! It stings! It stings! It hurts a ton! I reach blindly for the shaving-cream-covered towel and press it to my leg.

A minute later, still stinging, I pull the towel away and instantly get dizzy at the sight of the blood soaking it. I reach for the counter to catch myself, but my hand slides right off because of all the shaving cream. I fall backward, razor in one hand, bloody towel in the other. It's a miracle I don't hit my head on the bathtub or slice up my face with the razor as my arms flail around. I land square on my butt. Fortunately the bath mat saves me from direct contact with the hard tile floor.

Ten seconds later, Mom is knocking loudly on the door. "Everything okay in there?"

I shake out my limbs to make sure nothing's broken. "I'm fine, just slipped." If she pulled the towel out of the hole in the door, she'd have a perfect view of me splayed on the floor. Instead she just says, "You really need to be more careful, Rory."

As soon as I hear her go back downstairs, I limp into my room, a new towel pressed against my leg, and call Annabelle. I know she told me to text her, but I only have one hand. She answers, and I can hear people talking and laughing in the background. Before she has a chance to tell me she can't talk, I say, "I used the razor. I'm bleeding. A lot. What do I do?"

"What did the babysitting book tell us to do about bleeding?"

"I didn't read that part."

"Did you put water on your leg before putting on the shaving cream? You did use the shaving cream, right?"

"Yes, I used it; no, I didn't wet my leg first. Was I supposed to? It hurts!"

"Did you shave your leg up, and not down?"

"Yes and no. First up, then down."

"Didn't you read the instructions on the can?"

"There are instructions? And don't yell at me. I'm in pain here."

"Okay, I just found the babysitting book. It says to clean it off with cold water, and then hold a towel over it until the bleeding stops."

"Okay."

"It also says if it doesn't stop in ten minutes, you might need stitches."

I look at my clock. It's probably been a good six minutes already.

"And it says to elevate it. That means lift it up."

I thank her and also mutter that she never should have left me, then limp back to the bathroom. I wish I'd wiped the shaving cream off first, because I've left a trail leading from the bathroom to my room, and back again. Once I've stuck my leg under the bathtub faucet to rinse off the remaining shaving cream, it is easier to assess the damage. Seems like I managed to peel a few layers of skin off the inside of my left calf. The skin is actually hanging there, mocking me.

On the positive side, the swath of leg directly next to the gash is nearly hair free.

Eight Band-Aids later, I've pretty much managed to hold the skin back in place. But as soon as I put my leg down, the blood starts flowing again and I have to peel all the Band-Aids off and keep pressing the wet towel to it. Who knew legs bled so easily? After about ten more minutes (and two more towels), the blood finally stops. The only Band-Aids left now are Sawyer's, which means my leg is a collage of Saturday morning cartoons. Bugs Bunny on top, followed by Big Bird, Tigger, Dora, Diego, Garfield, and Snoopy.

And I'm no closer to those smooth, silky legs I'll need for the soccer scene tomorrow. In fact, I'm considerably further away. The box of wax catches my eye. The slogans on the front proclaim: PAIN-FREE WAXING! NO BURNING! LONG LASTING! ALL NATURAL! The words *all natural* don't impress me anymore, but I like the pain-free, no-burning part. I shove the towels all the way to the bottom of the laundry bin. The bathroom window reveals Mom watching Sawyer out back in his sandbox, which means the kitchen is free for at least a little longer. According to the instructions on the box, I only need to heat the wax for two minutes.

The gash is on the inner part of my leg, so if I walk too quickly, it rubs up against my other calf. This is not good. This hurts like heck. I have to walk very carefully and slowly, which is frustrating, because Sawyer's short attention span to any activity means he could get bored of the sandbox at any minute and lead Mom back inside. Once the rest of my legs are hair free, she'll be so impressed she won't bother to question me about the bloody gash.

When I finally make it to the kitchen, I carefully peel off the plastic and stick the container of wax in the microwave. Dad always says *A watched pot never boils*, and usually I agree with him. But the timer on the microwave is ticking down the seconds SO SLOWLY and I really, REALLY don't want Mom to walk in right now.

I stop the microwave a few seconds before it can make its loud beep, grab the container, and hobble away as fast as I can, which is to say, very slowly. They must be right about the "no burning" part, because the container only feels mildly warm. Back upstairs in the bathroom, I make a point of reading the directions over *twice*, then spread a new towel out on the floor and ease my way down. A thin wooden spatula and strips of gauze fall out of the box when I turn it upside down. According to the directions, I have to slather on a thin layer of the wax, lay one of the gauze strips on top of it, press firmly along the length of it, grab one end, and quickly tear it off. Sounds painful, but the lady on the box is smiling as she reveals her hair-free legs, and that gives me hope.

I scoop up some of the wax with the spatula and slowly bring it over to my non-injured leg. The wax has a pleasant smell, sort of like toasted marshmallows. I'm prepared to flinch as it makes contact with my skin, but it's not hot, only warm and sort of comforting. I spread it upward, then add a little more to cover the spaces that the spatula skipped over. It's not as easy to get the gauze to cover the stripe of wax exactly, and I have to push and pull it in a few directions, trying not to bunch it up too much. Maybe I took too long, and the wax hardened. I don't know. But when I rip the gauze off, it feels like my entire leg is on fire. I gasp at the pain and watch as it turns bright red right in front of my eyes.

Are those . . . *blisters?*

This is *so* not good. I manage to stand and hobble out to the hallway. Swallowing my pride and summoning my strength, I yell, "Mom!"

"What is it, Rory?" she calls from downstairs. "I'm making dinner."

"There's been an . . . *incident,*" I call down, borrowing her own expression.

She comes running, Sawyer at her heels. I try not to wince from the throbbing. Her eyes widen when she sees my leg — the red, blistery one — and then widen even more when she sees the one with all the Band-Aids. She quickly pushes Sawyer behind her legs, but he ducks around her. His mouth opens in a silent scream when he sees the damage I've inflicted.

"You're traumatizing your brother," my mother scolds, ushering Sawyer into his bedroom.

"What about me?" I shift my weight, and grimace. "I'm pretty traumatized, too!"

"Look on the bright side. Now no one will notice your puffy face."

"You always know how to make me feel better, Mom," I say, wincing as I try to turn around.

"C'mon, let's bandage up that leg," she orders, helping me shuffle back into the bathroom.

First she puts antiseptic on it, which almost makes me jump out of my skin. Then she gently coats it with some kind of ointment and wraps a gauze bandage around it, securing it with surgical tape. Good thing we have a well-stocked first aid kit! When she's done, she stands back to admire her handiwork. I'm glad I hid the bloody towels so she won't realize how bad the other leg is.

"Can you make it back to your room?"

Since both legs hurt now, the only way I can walk is with really wide steps, like a cowboy who's sat on a horse for too long. With her help, I make it to my bed and lie flat on my back.

"You've had a tough couple of days. What can I do to help?"

"You could do my homework for me tonight."

"What else ya got?"

I'm momentarily distracted by the fact that both my legs are throbbing in tune with my heartbeat. She repeats her question. I turn my head toward her and say, "Well . . . you could get me the bunny from the pet store. A bunny would REALLY cheer me up."

She laughs and walks toward the door. "I'll think about it."

"It's on the chart!" I call after her.

After a few minutes of staring at the ceiling, I reach out my arm and feel around on the bed for my phone. I have to scoot over about a foot to reach it, making little *ow* sounds every inch or two. A text is waiting from Annabelle.

<ARE U OK NOW? I DID MY LEGS, TOO. I USED THE LOTION STUFF THAT U SPREAD ON, WAIT 10 MINUTES, AND RUB OFF. IT SMELLED PRETTY BAD, BUT ALL THE HAIR IS GONE. TOO BAD I GRABBED THAT ONE WHEN I LEFT.>

YEAH. I text back. THAT REALLY IS TOO BAD.

She's your best friend, I tell myself as I let the phone flop out of my hand onto the bed. *She didn't mean to stick you with the bad stuff.* I stare up at the ceiling and listen to Mom comforting Sawyer in his bedroom.

I wish I had Throckmorton to comfort *me*. I consider getting him out of the box in the closet, but it would be too much effort to walk over there. Plus, curling up with my teddy bear isn't very mature for a leg-shaving twelve-year-old.

Instead, I comfort myself by focusing on how nice my one hair-free stripe is.

Chapter Twelve

"Omigod!" Annabelle runs over as soon as she sees my mom helping me out of the car. And to think, I used to be embarrassed by my mom simply *dropping me off*. At least she let me wear sweatpants to school, which is something I never get to do. But they're the only pants loose enough to be comfortable.

"What happened?" Annabelle asks as I hobble by, doing my cowboy walk. "Did you fall off your bike or something?"

I stare at her, trying to quell my rising anger at her question. "My legs? The razor? The waxing?"

"Oh, right! Duh, sorry!" She slips my bag off my shoulder and swings it onto her own.

How can I be mad at a person who does something thoughtful like that? Although when I look down at her hair-free, blood-free, and blister-free legs, it gets harder to be forgiving.

"Are you going to be okay?" she asks.

People throw sideways glances at me as we walk down the hall. Probably because I'm moving at, like, one mile an hour. "I'm sure I'll survive."

"Look on the bright side." She grins. "Now people won't notice your face anymore."

"You know, you and my mom should really hang out more."

"Hey, what about the movie today? You have to wear shorts, and like, run around and stuff."

We have to squeeze past a group of crew members setting up equipment, and my legs rub against each other. I grimace and say, "I know. I guess I have to tell that Brenda lady that I won't be able to go."

Annabelle stops walking to stare at me in disbelief. I know it would mean I'd lose the job, but what other choice do I have? She opens her mouth to argue, but starts frantically pointing behind me instead. Before I can figure out why she's acting so weird, I hear a boy's voice say, "Definitely a one today."

I'd recognize that voice anywhere. I hold my breath and turn. He's smiling. "A one, you know, your face. I had an allergic reaction last summer. We were shooting out in a field, and a bee stung me. My face swelled up like a pumpkin. Everyone stared at me, too, so I know how you feel."

For the millionth time, I wish I knew if a one was good or bad on the one to ten scale. I'm hoping it's good. Jake is flanked on both sides by security guards who already look bored. He's wearing a black T-shirt and jeans and his teeth are so white I can't believe they're real. So I'm supposed to talk to him now? How am I supposed to do that? Annabelle kicks me and I can't help it, I grab my leg and scream. That's one way to get out of talking!

"Oops!" Annabelle says, throwing her hand over her mouth. "I'm sorry, I forgot!"

"What's wrong?" Jake asks, glancing down at my leg in concern. "Are you hurt?"

I force a smile on my face and say, "Just an old war wound acting up. I'll be fine."

He laughs. "Good. Well, see you guys on the field." With a wink at Annabelle, he says, "Try to keep your friend out of harm's way."

"Oh, I will. See you later!"

He and his oversized buddies walk away, and I watch him stop occasionally to comment to other kids. What a nice guy!

Annabelle smacks me on the arm. "Old *war wound*? Where did *that* come from?"

I rub my arm. I don't think Annabelle knows her own strength. "I heard my dad say it once when he didn't want to explain why he was limping."

"Why was he limping?"

"He stepped on one of Sawyer's toy soldiers, and his foot got all infected with pus."

"That's gross."

"That's why he didn't want to tell people."

"Do you realize Jake Harrison just told us he'd see us later?" she says, reaching out to grab me, but I step out of the way of her killer grip.

"I know! I guess I'm going to the filming after all!"

"You sure are!"

We reach my homeroom, and Annabelle hands me my bag. Before I go in, I say, "Hey, did you hear from Sari last night? I hope she's okay."

"Omigod, she didn't tell you?" Annabelle asks. "She IM-ed me late last night!"

"Tell me what?"

The bell rings, and we both jump. As she backs away, she says, "She got a job working in the makeup trailer!"

"WHAT? How?"

"Long story, she'll have to tell you at lunch."

But Sari doesn't show up for lunch, so Annabelle fills me in. "Okay, so you know how Sari didn't get picked to be an extra?"

I don't bother to answer, since obviously I know that. Annabelle takes a sip of her soda and continues. "So after she left the gym, she went to scope out the trailers and starts chatting with this one lady who works in the hair and makeup trailer. The lady was super-impressed with how much Sari knew about hair, and said they could use an assistant. She's gonna get five bucks an hour!"

We keep watching the cafeteria doors for Sari, but the bell rings and she never shows up. Turns out she had snuck out to the trailer at lunch, a fact I learn during gym class. She tells me that the makeup ladies don't think very much of Madison. "They gossip right in front of me!" She shakes her head at the wonder of it all. "How cool is that?"

Before I can answer, she launches into a detailed description of all the beauty supplies in the trailer, and how the ladies told her they have to use this really heavy powder on Madison because of her acne scars. She's describing the rows of hairbrushes when the gym teacher blows the whistle, and she hops up to join the volleyball game. That girl is a ball of energy. Getting out of gym is the first positive thing to come out of my injuries. All I had to do was show the gym teacher one of my legs and she waved me over to the bleachers.

By the time school is over, the pain has faded a bit. They feel less *raw.* I'm still moving slowly, though, so by the time I get to the locker room to change for the filming, everyone is already gone. When I slip off my sweats, the sight takes me by surprise. My legs might feel better, but they sure don't look better. In fact, they look like something out of a horror movie. I quickly slip on my shorts and head out to the field. Cameras with big microphones dangling off the front of them are scattered around, with crew members darting every which way. I can't help noticing that the field has never looked better. Freshly planted grass, newly painted white lines on the football field. Even the wooden bleachers have been sanded and repolished.

I join the other extras behind the goalpost. With so many people, it's easy to hide in the back. And Annabelle is kind enough to stand directly in front of me whenever possible. It's fun to watch the action on the field as the director is blocking out the scene. Then Jake and Madison arrive, along with a group of other actors who will have speaking roles in the movie. I recognize two of them from guest-starring roles on TV shows. Jake and Madison are both wearing soccer uniforms, and look much better than any of the rest of us in our dorky gym clothes. Madison's hair is pulled back perfectly into a high ponytail, which makes her look even prettier, if that's possible. One of the PAs runs up and spritzes Madison in the face with a water bottle. I expect her to freak out, but she just closes her eyes and lets the girl spritz away.

Annabelle leans in and whispers, "Movie stars don't sweat, they glow."

Finally, Brenda comes over and tells us it's time. Day One of filming *Playing It Cool!* is about to begin! She demonstrates the exercises we'll be doing when the scene starts shooting. Jumping jacks, relays, that sort of thing. Fortunately she doesn't make us practice because time is short. We line up in rows (I take the back), and when she yells, "Action!" we begin our jumping jacks. I can see the cameras are trained on the action happening on the field, but the shot must be picking us up, too. I'll never watch a movie the same way again.

Each time my legs move in and out, I feel a renewed sense of jealousy that Annabelle got the wipe-away lotion and I got, well, the stuff that pulls your skin off. I feel a little tickle on my left leg. To my horror, a drop of blood has leaked out right next to Garfield's head. If I stop moving, I could risk messing up the whole scene. All I can do is hope it doesn't start running down my leg. After about five minutes of jumping (and, for me at least, *praying*), the director yells, "Cut!" Brenda walks the line, giving us pointers for the next shot. Apparently they now have to film it from the opposite angle, so we have to do the jumping jacks all over again. When she gets to me, she says, "Geez, what happened to you?"

The war wound line doesn't seem appropriate, so I just swallow hard and say, "Little shaving accident."

"Yeah, well, now it's a little soccer accident." She waves a crew member over and tells him to grab a doctor's coat from the wardrobe trailer. Before I know it, I'm being hustled over to the sidelines and told to sit on the grass. A "doctor" is bending down next to me, pretending to examine my leg. The "doctor" is my history teacher, Mr. Matthews, who had been walking to his car when he was recruited.

Brenda calls one of the cameramen over and instructs him to film some footage of the two of us fake-talking, and him fake-wrapping. She sticks a soccer ball under my arm to lend credibility. Like I just love soccer so much that even when I get hurt I can't part with the ball? Also, it's very strange to have your history teacher holding your leg. Especially if it's mutilated and hairy.

But I can't complain too much, because I'm so close to Jake and the others now that I can hear their dialogue on the field. From what I can pick up, Jake is the new kid in town, trying out for the school soccer team. Madison is the captain of the girls' team and doesn't want him to get picked for reasons we don't know yet. No one is breaking into song, or running onto the field in a scary mask, so I'm thinking teen comedy/drama is probably the best bet. They film the scene over and over again, although it always looks the same to me. The extras have moved on to relays. Most of them look like they're ready to keel over.

My stomach is starting to rumble by the time the director booms, "It's a wrap!" into his megaphone. The "doctor" helps me up and I wait for Annabelle before heading back to the locker room to grab our stuff. She reaches me right as the actors are leaving the field. We watch as Madison slips her hand possessively into Jake's. We're not the only ones to notice this. Behind me I hear a gasp, then an *oof* sound. I turn in time to see Annabelle helping Kira off the ground. She had tripped over her own feet. The commotion causes Jake and Madison to look over at us. I try to hide behind Annabelle but I'm not fast enough.

"How are the legs?" Jake asks me.

Unable to answer, I just smile weakly. Madison looks from Jake to me, and her eyes search my face. I can tell she's trying to remember where she's seen me before. Then she glances at Kira, and I can see the memory has come back to her. She starts to laugh. "Jake, you've got to see the book this girl made, it's so funny you won't bel —"

I finally find my voice. "They look worse than they feel," I say loudly, still wishing more than anything that I had my sweats back on.

"That's good to hear," he says.

Madison glares at me, and pulls him away. Kira hurries away, too, in the opposite direction.

"Wow!" Annabelle says. "I think Madison Waters hates you!"

"I know, isn't that funny?" The girl no one ever notices is hated by a famous movie star. It's crazy! As we leave the field, one of the production assistants hands us each twenty dollars.

I can't wait to tell my parents all about the filming, but when I get home, they're acting strange. Even stranger than usual. Like they keep smiling, but then keep trying to pretend they're *not* smiling by looking all serious. Sawyer is so antsy he won't stop jumping from foot to foot. My face has pretty much returned to normal, so he's able to make eye contact again, which is good. I keep hearing all these banging and scraping noises, but I'm too busy telling them about the filming to pay much attention.

Eventually I get through the story, and Mom and Dad murmur all the right things like "wow" and "interesting" and "that sounds like fun!" Then Dad excuses himself to go work in the dining room, and Mom ushers a squirmy Sawyer into the other room and puts on his potty video, which quiets him right down.

After a dinner of pizza (with mashed-up carrots and peas hidden underneath the cheese that, as usual, Sawyer doesn't notice), I pretty much hide out in my room all night, catching up on homework. It's weird not having my parents over my shoulder asking me if it's finished and then going over it. But it's not like they could do that for the rest of my life. Mom comes into the bathroom while I'm brushing my teeth and offers to clean and re-dress my wounds. I get dizzy when I see them uncovered, so I stare at a spot on the ceiling until she's done. I'm so exhausted that I don't even care that my bedtime isn't officially for another half hour. I fall asleep as soon as my head hits the pillow.

So it's perfectly understandable that when I wake up an hour later to find two red, glowing eyes staring at me from across the room, I scream at the top of my lungs. Seriously, anyone would have.

Chapter Thirteen

I can just make out my parents' footsteps over the sound of my screams. Untangling myself from my blanket, I jump out of bed and race for the door. It takes a few seconds for the pain in my legs to kick in, but when it does, I stumble, lose my balance, and bump into something that I can't immediately identify in the dark, but that goes crashing to the floor with a *bam*.

I stand in the middle of my room, frozen, as my parents rush in and switch on my light. Blinking fast, I look around wildly for the source of the red eyes and the *bam*. The first thing I see is the floor, and the huge bag with the words RABBIT PELLETS printed in big, black letters. Then I see the rabbit pellets themselves, scattered to the far corners of the room. Rabbit pellets? Why on earth would a huge bag of rabbit pellets be in my room? Unless . . .

I twist around until I'm facing my dresser. Right there, right next to my old snowman lamp, is Kyle (now and forever known as Bunny) happily chomping away on a piece of lettuce.

Dad looks sheepish. "Um . . . surprise?"

I don't know whether to laugh or cry.

"We thought you'd see him when you woke up in the morning," Mom explains, gently leading me around the bag and over to the cage. "Guess we didn't really think it through."

"When . . . how . . . when did you get him?" I ask, feeling my heart swell as I watch his little nose move up and down while he eats.

"Sawyer and I picked him up this afternoon while you were filming your scene. I thought for sure Sawyer would give it away."

"But I thought you said I had to wait to get him?"

Dad puts his hand on my shoulder. "We think you're responsible enough to take care of him now. We paid for the initial expenses, and you'll have to cover the upkeep."

"I will," I promise, glancing over at the spilled food that I'll now have to replace. I really want to hold him, but I remember reading there's this whole process in getting them to bond with you. The middle of the night probably isn't the best time for that.

Mom helps me back to bed while Dad sweeps up the pellets. I gaze happily at Bunny until Dad switches off the light.

Boy, those red eyes sure do glow in the dark.

•   •   •   •   •   •   •   •   •   •   •   •

All I can think about at school is Bunny. I can't wait to get home to play with him. This morning he let me hold him and stroke his nose and ears and I fed him a piece of bread, which he loved. He is *soooooo* cute! Mom is taking me to the pet store after school so I can buy more pellets and some chew toys.

At lunch Sari brings us into the hair and makeup trailer. She has a badge around her neck, like the official crew members. It's VERY cool. All she does is flash the badge and the security people part and let us through. Annabelle immediately sits down in one of the makeup chairs and starts powdering her face with a big cotton puffball. I'm afraid to try any of the makeup.

"Look at this," Sari says, holding up a shiny white and green shirt. "It's part of the soccer uniform Jake wore in the scene yesterday." She brings it to her nose and sniffs deeply. I wrinkle my nose. I mean, I like Jake, too, but I don't feel the need to smell his sweat. She drapes it over her shoulder and then directs me into one of the chairs. Leaning over the counter, she plugs in a hair straightener and turns it on.

"My hair's already pretty straight," I point out.

She shakes her head. "This does more than just straighten your hair." She picks up a section of my hair, places it between the two halves of the straightener, and runs it down the length of it. I feel my hair when she's done. It's so smooth and silky, it feels like butter. "Wow! No wonder Madison's hair always looks so great."

Sari picks up another section, then glances out the small window above the mirror. She quickly tosses Jake's shirt back on the counter and grabs a tube of red lipstick out of Annabelle's hand. "C'mon," she urges. "We've gotta go!" She races down the steps of the trailer and takes off, followed by Annabelle. It's still not easy for me to move very quickly because of my legs, so I trail behind. I catch up a few feet away from the school.

"Hey," I say, panting from the effort. "What was that all about?"

"Yeah," Annabelle says. "I thought you were allowed to be there."

"Technically I'm not supposed to be there unless one of the hair and makeup ladies is around," Sari admits, glancing nervously back at the trailers.

I can see someone entering the one we just left.

"C'mon," Sari urges. "We need to get back inside before anyone sees us." She and Annabelle take off in a run toward the door in the courtyard that no one uses except the gardening club. It's the same one we snuck out through. It's locked from the outside, though, so we had to stick a rock in there to keep it open. I just wave them on. "Go. Save yourselves."

At least they're nice enough to leave the rock in the door so I don't have to find a window to crawl through.

The next time I see Sari again, in the locker room before gym, she pulls me into a corner of the changing area. She's all sweaty, and not in the glowy way that Madison was sweaty.

"What's wrong?" I ask.

"I'm on probation!" she whispers.

"What does *that* mean?"

"It means they knew I was in there. I went back after my Spanish class because I had this terrible feeling that I left the straightening iron on."

My eyes widen. "So what happened?"

"I walked in, and the three makeup ladies were all in there, and it smelled like smoke. I tried to back out, but they saw me and asked me, and I couldn't lie. Plus, the thing that caught fire? It was Jake's soccer uniform! I had left it on the counter with the iron."

"Wow!"

"I know! They had to throw it out and everything."

"So what happens now?"

"I have to be really good and not break any more rules."

"Can you do that?"

She nods. "I think so." Then she lowers her voice again and adds, "One good thing did come out of it."

"What?"

She reaches under her shirt and pulls out a wad of material. She unfurls it to reveal Jake's uniform, complete with scorch marks and a huge hole in the middle.

"Well, I'm glad to see you're not breaking any more rules."

· · · · · · · · · · · ·

When Mom picks me up from school, she announces we'll be dropping Sawyer off on the way for a playdate with a boy from his preschool class. Apparently this kid was potty trained at, like, six months, and she's hoping it'll rub off on Sawyer. They live in a part of town we don't go to very often, so it takes a while to find the house. Sawyer spends most of the ride singing an ode to Hot Lips that he made up off the top of his head.

We finally pull up to the curb, and Mom gathers Sawyer and his diaper bag from the back. "Wait here," she instructs.

"Where am I going to go?"

She disappears inside the house, and I daydream about Bunny and the games we're going to play when I get home. Not even a minute later, an elderly woman who reminds me of Grandma passes by, walking a big yellow dog. Actually, it's more like the dog is walking *her*. She's barely holding on. Then right while I'm watching, a squirrel darts across the street, and the dog takes off after it, barking and yanking the leash right out of the woman's hand. She stands there, clearly stunned, then starts after him. There's no way she'll catch up, though. She's not what you'd call spry.

I check the front door of the house Mom just went into, but it's still closed. Seeing no other option, I push my car door open and take off after the dog. I cut across two people's front yards, neatly dodging flower gardens and hedges, until I can step on the leash to make him stop. He halts in surprise, then surrenders and hangs his head. I lead him back into the street and wave to the woman, who is still half a block away. She stops when she sees me, and I bring the dog back to her.

"Thank you, young lady," she says, breathless. I hand her the leash, and she takes it with a trembling hand. "He's a feisty one."

"It was no problem. I could use the exercise."

Up close I can see she doesn't really look like Grandma, but she has the same kind smile. "Um, I better get back to my mom. She doesn't like me to talk to strangers on the street." Ugh, why did I say that to this nice old lady? Now I sound like a jerk.

But she just waves good-bye as the dog pulls her down the sidewalk again. I hurry back to the car and swing the door shut behind me just as Mom comes out of the house.

"Sorry that took so long," she says as she climbs in the car. "You know how I get leaving him at a new place."

"No problem." I want to tell her about the lady and the dog, but then she'd know I left the car. It's not until we're walking through the mall parking lot and my legs ache that I realize I hadn't even thought about them while I was running after the dog.

The manager of the pet store is out in front, piling up a pyramid of dog food cans. "Figured I'd see you today," he says as we enter. I turn around, assuming he's talking to someone behind me. But no one's there.

"Me?" I ask. "You knew I'd knock over the rabbit food?"

He looks from me to my mom, and back again. "You're here for more food?"

I nod. "I spilled most of it last night. Long story." I glance accusingly at my mom, who pretends not to notice.

"So everything's good with Kyle?" he asks, standing up to straighten the can on the top of the pyramid.

"Sure. I renamed him Bunny, though."

He chuckles at that, and I remind myself that he doesn't like rabbits. He shows us where the chew toys are, and then when we're ready to ring it all up, he tosses in a few free toys and some nibbling sticks. "On the house," he says with a wink.

Strange guy.

Mom carries the bag out of the store. She's used to carrying Sawyer around all the time, and he weighs a lot more than that bag. She stops in front of the ear-piercing store and sets it down on the floor.

"Do you need me to carry it the rest of the way?" I ask, kind of hoping she'll say no.

She shakes her head. "I thought maybe, since we're here, that you'd like to get your ears pierced today." She reaches into her pocket and pulls out Grandma's earrings! She must have slipped them out of my dresser drawer.

At first my heart leaps. My ears pierced! Finally! And then I remember that boy and the screaming. "Um, I'm not sure. . . ."

Mom almost drops the earrings in surprise. "You've been begging me since you were eight years old. What gives?"

I tell her about the teenage boy. She laughs. "Honey, men are wimps. Why do you think it's women who have the babies? C'mon, you'll be fine." She dangles the earrings in front of me. "They sure do bring out your eyes. . . ."

They really do. But I'd have to wear those starter earrings first anyway. "Maybe I should get the contacts today instead?"

She glances at her watch. "We need more time for that. So what do you say?"

I peer into the store window and see a six-year-old girl hop off the stool, smiling and holding her mom's hand. If she can do it and not even cry, Mom must be right about the men-being-wimps thing. "Okay, let's do it."

While Mom signs me up at the desk, I head over to the rack of starter earrings and pick out the gold balls. No one else is waiting, so Mom tells me it's my turn. The lady holding the piercing gun is the same one who was here last time. As I settle in the chair, I can't help asking about the boy and if he ever went through with the piercing. At first she seems not to remember who I'm talking about, and I wonder if that means a lot of kids wind up crying and leaving, and that makes me want to leave again.

"We offer ice to numb the ear first, and some kids — teenage boys especially — pass on the ice. You know, they want to tough it out."

"I'll take the ice," I say hurriedly. She smiles and reaches around to a little freezer. While she's pulling out the ice pack, Mom asks, "Can you tell me how you sterilize your equipment?"

The lady hands me a small ice pack in the shape of a cat's head, and brings my hand up to my right ear. Then she turns to Mom and says, "We clean the area with antiseptic before we begin, and then dab on some antibiotic cream afterward." She waves the metal thing around in the air. "And this is a single-use piercing gun. The only thing to actually make contact with the skin is the hypoallergenic gold stem of the earring." She turns back to me. "I'll be going over how to care for your ears, and will give you instructions to take home. You can always call with any questions."

Mom seems satisfied. My ear is getting cold.

"You ready?" the lady asks.

I lower the ice pack and nod. I'm tempted to reach for Mom's hand but don't want to look like a baby.

"Okay," she says. "First, I'm going to wipe your ear with the antiseptic, then I'll place a dot on the right spot." She leans over and takes my ear in her hand. I close my eyes. She fiddles around a little, but my ear is so numb I don't even feel the cotton ball or the pen touch it. I decide that, babyish or no, I want to hold my mom's hand. I open my eyes to reach for it, when Mom says, "It looks great, honey!"

How could a red dot look great? "What do you mean?"

"The earring!" she says, pointing to a mirror that the lady is holding up. "Look!"

To my amazement, there's a gold earring in my ear! I hadn't felt a thing, not even a pinch! The lady smiles at my reaction. "So I guess it wasn't too bad, huh?" she asks.

I grin, almost giddy with delight, switch the ice pack to my left hand, and move it up to my ear. While we wait for that one to get numb, the lady dabs some antibiotic ointment on the front and back of the newly pierced ear with a Q-tip. Now that the numbness is starting to wear off, I can feel a little twinge and a slight tugging sensation. Nothing too painful, though. A girl and her mom watch from the side, right where Annabelle and I stood the other day. The mother is holding the fake diamond starter earrings. The girl is a few years younger than me, and I can tell she's nervous by the way she keeps twisting her hair and biting it. I give her the thumbs-up sign, and she quickly lets the batch of hair fall. Laying the ice pack down in my lap, I say, "Okay, ready for the next one."

The lady picks up the red pen and walks over to my other side. I decide to close my eyes again since that worked out so well last time. Then I hear Mom say, "Um, is that normal?" and my heart sinks to the floor.

Reluctantly, I open my eyes to see Mom pointing at my ear. The one with the shiny new earring that makes me really happy and didn't hurt at all. I guess now that I think about it, there's a dull sort of *throbbing* going on now. The lady rests the piercing gun on the table and comes over to look. "Hmm, that's strange. You're not allergic to gold, are you?"

"Mom?" I ask, beginning to panic. "Am I?" It might be my imagination, but her face seems awfully pale all of a sudden.

Turning to the woman, she says, "I thought you said the earrings were hypoallergenic?"

"It's very rare to be allergic to gold," the lady insists. "This honestly never happens."

Where have I heard *that* before? I try to pick up the hand mirror, but Mom blocks me. "I think you better take the earring out."

The throbbing is worsening. I remember the girl in line with her mother and turn to look for them. They're nowhere in sight.

"I don't think I can," the lady says. "It's sort of . . . embedded in there."

"What?" my mom and I say at the same time. My hand flies up to my ear. At first I'm not sure what part of my ear I'm touching, but then I realize that the earlobe is so swollen it almost completely covers the earring, front and back. The next thing I know, I hear a sort of popping sound, and the back of the earring shoots right into my hand.

"Well!" the lady exclaims, shaking her head. "That's something you don't see every day."

"Can you pull the earring out from the front now?" Mom urges.

"I'll try," the lady says. But as soon as she touches my ear I cry out, and she jerks backward.

"Sorry," I mutter. "Just a little sensitive."

"We may have to wait for it to make its way out on its own."

While they stand there helplessly, I grab the mirror and instantly wish I hadn't. I look like Horton, that Dr. Seuss elephant with the huge ears. Except I have one huge ear, and one normal-sized ear. "What's that white stuff oozing out the sides of the hole? Please tell me that's the antibiotic you put on?"

She peers at my ear. "Um, no, I think that's pus." I actually drop the mirror, and she dives for it, catching it only a few inches away from hitting the floor. "Pus is a *good* thing," she claims, replacing the mirror on the small table. "It means your body is recognizing a foreign object and is fighting it off."

"Yay, me," I reply weakly. I'm feeling dizzy from seeing the pus. The throbbing isn't helping.

The lady turns to my mom and says, "Why don't you go to the smoothie stand across the hall and ask for some crushed ice. I'll put it in a baggie, and that way the ice can bend around her ear." Mom nods, squeezes my hand, and runs out.

We wait in an awkward silence. "So," I say, "I guess you don't want to try the other ear?"

She shakes her head and says something I can't quite make out. My earlobe has now puffed up so much that it's covering the opening to my ear. I caught the words *antiseptic, antibacterial,* and *at home,* so I think I got the important stuff. Allergic to *gold*? What kind of girl is allergic to gold? My spirits sag even further when I realize

I won't be able to wear Grandma's earrings now. Maybe not ever.

Mom returns and the ice is transferred into a small baggie. I hold it around my ear. It hurts if I press too hard, though, so I'm not really sure it's helping anything. The piercing lady promises that the swelling should go down really quickly, and that once I can pry the earring out, I'll feel much better. A teenage boy comes in, sees me, blanches, and scurries back out. I want to tell him to man up, but I'd run away from me, too, if I could.

The lady refunds our money without even being asked, and sort of rushes us out of the store without trying to look like that's what she's doing.

I feel wobbly as we walk out, like I'm going to tip over. "I think your balance is a little off," Mom says, taking my arm with the hand that isn't holding the pet food bag. "Your inner ear controls your equilibrium. You better lie low until it heals."

"Please speak into my good ear."

She repeats what she said, but into my left ear. "We still have time before we have to get Sawyer; let's swing by the doctor's office."

Oh, joy.

Besides the mothers, I'm the oldest by about eight years at the pediatrician's office. All the little kids gawk at me when we walk into the waiting room, and I wonder why no one has told them that it's not polite to stare. One of the women pulls her son close to her as we take our seats. Mom sees this and says, "She's not contagious. I'm more concerned about what *he's* going to give *her.*"

You tell her, Mom! I wish I had a book to hide my face behind, but I have to settle for some old *Highlights* magazines from my mom's generation.

"Yep, you're allergic to gold," the doctor says when it's our turn. "And from what your mom told me on the phone the other day, you should stay away from plant-based products as well. Down the road we'll send you for more extensive testing to try to narrow down the culprit." Then I have to hold still while he uses this tool that looks like a skinny pair of pliers to pull the earring out. I do my best not to scream, but a small one might have escaped.

I'm about to hop off the table when he says, "Hang on. I'd like to give you an allergy shot before you leave. It's more effective than the liquid, and since you're just coming off the other allergic reaction, I think it's a good idea."

I glare at my mom even though I know this whole thing's not her fault. On the other hand, maybe it is! After all, she *made* me, which means I can blame my plant sensitivity and gold allergy on her.

As he readies the shot, Mom says, "While we're here, can you take a look at her legs?"

"What's wrong with her legs?"

Will the humiliation never end? Having no choice, I lift up my pant legs and show him.

He peeks under the bandages. "Oh, my." Fortunately he doesn't pry, just gives Mom a handful of ointment packets and tells me to put clean bandages on each night for a week. He points to my left leg. "You might have a scar on that one."

Great. So now I'll have a lifelong reminder of the whole experience.

"Well, Mom," I say, rubbing my upper arm as we climb into the car, "this has been a really fun day. Thanks."

"Look on the bright side," she replies. "Now no one will notice you're walking funny."

"Ha-ha. If this motherhood gig doesn't work out, you could take your act on the road."

She laughs and says, "Don't tempt me. Hey, and when I pick up Sawyer, try to cover your ear with your hair."

The only thing that makes me feel better is knowing that Bunny is waiting for me at home. I cover my ear the best I can, and Sawyer's so tired from his playdate that he doesn't notice anything. I don't think I could stand to hear him screaming again. Even with my one good ear.

Dad opens the door before I even step up on the porch. The breeze has blown my hair away from my ear and his jaw drops when he sees me. Mom walks up with Sawyer just as Dad opens his mouth, and she gives him a quick shake of her head. He closes his mouth and clears his throat. "Ah, you got a phone call, Rory. It was the AD for the movie. She said she tried to call your cell, but it wouldn't accept the call. I'll program it in for you tonight."

"What did she want?" I ask, wondering if I could be in trouble somehow. Maybe they found out Annabelle and I were in the trailer with Sari, and they're firing us? I really hope not, since I just spent all the money from the soccer game scene at the pet store.

"She said they need all the extras tomorrow after school. You'll need to bring party clothes with you."

"Perfect," I mumble. Not only do I *not* have party clothes, I have an elephant's ear. I grab the pet store bag and storm up the stairs. Well, as much as I *can* storm. I fling open my bedroom door and the first thing I see is Bunny's cage on my dresser. The second thing I see is that it's empty.

This is not good. I look all around the cage, my desk, the floor.

Nothing. No Bunny.

I also don't hear any nibbling or crunching, but that

might be because of my sudden deafness in one ear. I double-check that the computer wires are still in one piece. My research told me rabbits love to chew wires, and they can get electrocuted that way.

Then I see him. He's sitting on my pillow, happily nibbling on a carrot he must have carried out of the cage in his mouth. I breathe a sigh of relief, and join him on the bed. I stroke his back for a few minutes and then text Annabelle and Sari to tell them what happened at the mall. Annabelle writes back first.

<THEY REALLY SHOULDN'T LET YOU OUT OF THE HOUSE. EVER.>

Sari's response is more helpful. <DON'T WORRY! I'LL GET YOU A HAT FROM THE WARDROBE TRAILER. AND I'M SURE IT'S NOT THAT BAD.>

If I didn't have the world's dorkiest phone, I could take a picture of my ear and send it. But since I *do* have the world's dorkiest phone, they'll just have to take my word for it.

Mom lets me eat dinner up in my room, since there's no way I could keep my hair over my ear the whole time. And the only hats we have in the house are baseball hats, which wouldn't cover it.

I spend the rest of the evening alternating between feeling sorry for myself, icing my elephant ear, and playing with Bunny. He loves tossing the chew toys up in the air and letting them fall on his head. I still don't know how he escaped. Dad swears he didn't let him out, and the door to his cage was still latched. Just to be on the safe side, after I hug him good night, I wind some tape around the latch.

Since I usually sleep on the side of my bad ear, it takes a while to get comfortable. Bunny must be having trouble, too, because he keeps turning around in his cage and nudging at his water dish. Once I fall asleep, I have this dream where an elephant is standing on my chest, pushing down on me. I can't breathe! I struggle against his foot, grunting and gasping for air, but he doesn't budge. Finally, I wake up out of the nightmare. As I lie there, trying to recover from the dream, I realize that even though I'm awake, I'm still having trouble breathing. Fear flows through me as I attempt to fill my lungs, and can't. I try to sit up, but it feels like that elephant from my dream is squeezing the air out of my chest. Panicking, I look down. There IS something pushing down on my chest. But it's not an elephant.

Chapter Fourteen

"*Your bunny is not trying to kill you,*" *Mom assures* me, pouring some Cheerios into my bowl.

"How can you be sure?" I can still feel his weight crushing my lungs.

"I'm pretty sure bunnies are nonviolent creatures."

From the other room Sawyer yells, "Bugs Bunny is the best!"

"Yes, he is, honey," Mom yells back. She's still keeping Sawyer away from me, due to my ear. I'm starting to miss him. It's a sad state of affairs when you can't be around your little brother because you scare him.

I guess in the light of day it seems pretty silly to accuse Bunny of any evildoings. He was probably just trying to snuggle close to me. It's not his fault those red eyes are so beady and scary in the dark.

Mom comes up behind me with a brush and some hair bands. She pushes my hair this way and that, trying to find a way to cover my ear. It's a little better this morning, more like a baby elephant's ear than a full-grown one's.

"I've really gotta go," I tell her, gathering my books from the table. "I'm meeting Sari early."

She steps back. "Okay, take a look."

A little wary of what I'll find, I head over to the mirror in the hallway. Basically I now have a single ponytail hanging down the side of my head. She gathered the hair just below my ear, so it sort of puffs up around it. "Well, it does hide my ear."

"It might not exactly be the hottest style," Mom admits. "But maybe you'll start a new trend."

"Probably not."

"Probably not," she agrees.

. . . .

"What's going on with the side ponytail?" Sari shrieks when she sees me. We had arranged to meet at the entrance to the trailer area before school. Her own hair is three inches shorter on one side, but on her it looks cool. "Let's get you in there before anybody sees you!" She ushers me past security by waving her badge, and practically throws me into the chair. I wave meekly at the two hair and makeup ladies who are busy setting things up for the day.

"Careful," I warn Sari as she's about to yank out the ponytail. "It's really sensit — ow! I asked you to be careful!"

"Sorry," she says. "Yikes, that looks pretty bad."

"That's why I was wearing the ponytail!"

"Trust me, a hat will be better." She digs through a box full of hats and scarves, but discards one after the other. While she digs, she says, "You know, Natalie's party is in two weeks. Do you think you could try not to maim yourself for that long?"

"I'll try," I promise.

"Try this one," one of the makeup ladies says, tossing me what appears to be a chef's hat.

"She might stand out a bit in that one," the other lady says. "You know, since this is a school and not the kitchen of a restaurant."

I'm glad she said it so I didn't have to. I lay the hat on the countertop.

"How about this one?" Sari asks, picking a white woolen cap off a hook. She plops it on my head, then pulls down the side to cover the offending ear. The four of us look at my reflection, and all shrug at almost exactly the same time. "Well, it does the job," Sari says, summing it up.

I can hear the warning bell ring over at the school, which must mean that my hearing is getting better. Sari and I are gathering our things to go when the trailer door bangs open. Madison and Jake walk in, laughing. Even without her makeup on, Madison is beautiful. I don't see any acne scars, either. She stops laughing when she sees us, but Jake keeps smiling that bright smile of his. Seriously, his teeth rival the clouds in whiteness.

"Nice hat!" he says. "It's, um, *jaunty*!"

Instinctively I reach up and touch it.

"Hey," Madison says, looking from the hat to the empty hook on the wall. "Isn't that my hat for the scene at the homecoming game?"

No one seems to know the answer to this.

"And why does it look so . . . *lumpy*?" Madison holds out her hand. "I'd like my hat, please."

"I really think she needs to wear it today," Sari says.

"Oh, you do?" Madison says. Then in two quick steps she's in front of me and tugging the cap right off my head. I grimace as it catches under my ear. For an instant everything's quiet as my ear is revealed. Then Jake bursts out laughing.

"You just can't catch a break, girl, can you?"

I shake my head sadly.

"Does it hurt?"

I glance at Sari, who is clearly mortified for me. "A little," I admit. "Especially" — I pause to glare at Madison — "when someone pulls at it."

She scowls. "Well, how was I supposed to know?"

"How did it happen?" Jake asks.

"Allergic reaction to a gold earring," I mumble.

"You're kidding!" he says.

I shake my head.

"Well, look on the bright side —"

I interrupt. "Don't say now no one will notice my face. Or my legs, whichever."

"I wasn't going to. I was just gonna say that on the bright side, your boyfriend's a lucky guy — he never has to buy you gold jewelry!"

The makeup ladies laugh. Madison just looks annoyed. I, however, am in shock. Does Jake really think *I* would have a *boyfriend*?

"C'mon," Sari says, tugging at my sleeve. "We're going to be late."

Still buzzing over Jake's words, I let her lead me out. We're halfway down the steps when the hat comes sailing after us. "Just take it," Madison snaps before turning on her heel.

Sari picks it up and sets it back on my head. It must have gotten stretched out or something, because it keeps slipping down all the way into school. Not too many people in Willow Falls wear hats in the middle of May. Or at any other time, really. I think the hat is attracting more attention than my ear would. So I pull it off and stuff it in my locker and hope for the best. I try to lie low and keep my hair over it as much as possible. By lunchtime, though, I decide maybe the hat's a better idea after all, and retrieve it from my locker. Before heading to the cafeteria, I duck into the bathroom to change into the clothes Annabelle brought me for the dance scene after school. The top fits pretty well, and the pink color matches my pink-colored ear, which while not something I want to play up, still sort of amuses me. The miniskirt is too long on me, but at least the leggings cover up my bandages. I'm stuck wearing my own shoes because her feet are bigger.

"Lose the hat," the director orders as Annabelle and I arrive at the gym after school. It's been transformed with streamers and balloons, and a big band is setting up on one end.

I gather up my nerve and say, "Um, I'm not sure I should. . . ."

"Why not?" he barks, checking a little video screen in his hand.

I lift the hat off my ear.

"Keep the hat," he commands. "Just stay in the background. *Far* in the background."

I nod, and we scurry to the bleachers to join the other extras. I actually need to go put more ointment on my ear, so I tell Brenda I'll be right back and hurry to the girls' locker room. I've only made it to the gym teacher's office when I hear the yelling. "I told you it's the role of a lifetime!" Madison's unmistakable voice shouts. "How could you turn it down?"

I duck into the empty office and hold my breath.

"Because I'm tired of playing the same guy in every movie," Jake explains. His voice is loud, too, but not as loud as hers. "I want to challenge myself. I want to explore my craft. I'm not like you. I don't want everyone following me all the time, just waiting for me to mess up or whatever."

Madison groans. "Why are we even bothering to do this? Here, take the ring. I can't even *fake*-date you anymore."

"Are you fake-breaking-up with me?" he asks, sounding amused.

"Yes!" she says, sounding anything *but* amused. She storms past me, thankfully not looking into the office. He follows a minute later, pushing the ring deep into his front pocket.

I let out my breath and hurry into the locker room. There's more drama *behind* the scenes of the movie than there is in the movie! By the time I finish and get back out, half of the extras have been placed in different parts of the gym. Annabelle waves to me from the dance floor, which, as far as I can tell from all the tape marks on the floor, is where a lot of the action will be taking place. The rest of the kids are either seated at the round tables, standing at the food table, or posed in small groups. Brenda calls off a few more names and directs them where to go. When she consults her list and says, "Rory?" I stand up. But so does Boy Rory. We look at each other and quickly sit down. "Sorry," we both mutter. Brenda points to Boy Rory and tells him to join the extras on the dance floor. Then she tells me to sit at the table farthest away from the dance floor, and to keep my bad ear always facing *away* from the camera.

I nod and take my new seat, which is only a few feet away from the crew and the video monitors. Amanda Ellerby is at my table, along with Kira and two seventh grade boys who never would have noticed me before, but who now stare at me as though they've never seen anyone with a baby elephant's ear. I wish I could text Annabelle and tell her what I overheard between Jake and Madison, but the director has a strict no-texting-on-the-set rule. Brenda comes over and tells us to start working on our fake-talking and fake-laughing. I don't feel much like laughing. The two boys pair off, so Amanda and Kira and I fake-talk, which is really hard with three people because you never know who you should be looking at. After a while, we give up and start real-talking instead. Since I can't talk to Annabelle and Sari, I decide to share what I overheard with them. Kira practically faints, like, she seriously turns pale and her eyes flutter. "They broke up?" she says, her voice catching at the end.

"Well, they were never really going out, right?" Amanda says.

"Right. It was all for publicity."

"Boy, the tabloids would love this!"

"We can't tell anyone, though," I insist, questioning my decision to tell them in the first place. "It wouldn't be fair."

"Don't worry," Amanda says. "I know how to keep a secret."

We both turn to look at Kira. But she's in her own world. The director finally starts shooting the scene, and we switch back to our fake-talking. It's actually kind of fun pretending we're having a conversation. I decide I like Amanda. She's fun. Kira is still sort of shaking, so she just pretends to keep sipping from her fake soda. Well, I guess it's *real* soda, but she's not really supposed to drink it.

Since we're so far in the back, we can't hear what the actors are saying on the dance floor. But we can hear what the crew says about it. Apparently everything was going fine until Madison refused to kiss Jake, which she was supposed to do at the end of the last song. Then Madison storms past us, followed by the director and Brenda. Brenda stops near our table to discuss the options with the crew. Amanda and I scoot our chairs over a few inches to hear better.

"We're almost done with the footage," Brenda says, consulting a screen. "We just need the kiss. It doesn't even have to be her face, we can do a back-of-the-head shot and digitize the rest of her later. But you-know-who has decided she no longer wants to kiss her fake boyfriend."

Amanda and I exchange surprised glances. So the crew knew all along! Then it hits me. I jump out of my chair and hurry up to Brenda. "Sorry for eavesdropping, but if you can do a back-of-the-head kiss, then how about just using someone else with dark hair?"

Brenda looks skeptical, but the other crew members nod. "That could work," one of the guys says.

Brenda turns to me and says, "I assume you're going to suggest yourself? And, no offense, but that" — she points to my ear — "would be hard to digitize out."

I shake my head. "Not me. Her." I point to Kira, who is still pretending to sip from her cup even though the director yelled *cut* ten minutes ago. "Her hair is much more like Madison's. In fact, from the back, if Kira were standing on a box, they might as well be the same person!"

Okay, I might have gone a little far on that last part, but Brenda goes off to consult with the director, who has returned from his apparently unsuccessful visit with Madison. I can't hear what they're saying, but it looks heated. Finally, they both nod, and Brenda comes over. She snaps her fingers in front of Kira and says, "Stand up. Time to make your dreams come true."

Kira, clueless, follows her obediently. Amanda turns to me. "Wow. I can't believe you did that. You could be the one kissing him."

"Nah. The ear, hat, and everything."

"Uh-huh," she says, unconvinced.

The kiss is being filmed on the other side of the gym, so we can't even catch a glimpse of it if we stand on the table, which we try as soon as we're sure the director can't see us. Since everyone else has to stay in their assigned spots, too, no one really figures out what's going on until one of the crew members yells out, "Watch out, she's gonna hit the floor!" a split second before we hear a *thump*. I've got to hand it to Kira, though. According to a report from Leo, who was only a few feet away from the action, after Kira fainted, she brushed herself off and got right back up on that step stool. Fifteen minutes and six (I'm sure not very painful) takes later, the director finally yells, "That's a wrap!" and everyone claps. Well, everyone except for Madison. But judging by the fact that after the director wrapped the scene, Kira fainted again, I'm pretty sure Madison doesn't have to worry about being permanently replaced anytime soon.

•   •   •   •   •   •   •   •   •   •   •

After the big dance night, the next few movie scenes take place in various hallways before or after school, where all we have to do is fake-talk at our lockers or pretend like we're hurrying to class. Thankfully, over the course of the week, my ear has become human-sized again, and Brenda is finally able to stop positioning me with my back to the camera.

The twenty-dollar bills from each scene are piling up nicely. It's really a great gig. I'm going to miss it when it ends.

I've already spent five dollars of my movie earnings on extra thick tape for Bunny's cage. He definitely can't chew through it, because each morning he's still in there, just as I left him. He's been very sweet, too, and I feel guilty for any mean thoughts I may have had, or any accusations I may have flung his way. Sawyer really likes him, too, and I think the feeling's mutual. Bunny thumps his back paws a lot when Sawyer is around, which I'm pretty sure is a sign of affection and trust.

Cleaning out the "droppings" isn't very fun, but it's a lot better than changing diapers. And so what if I have to move his cage to the floor at night so I can't see his red glowing eyes staring at me out of the darkness? Small price to pay for his cuteness during the day.

On Saturday morning, Mom knocks on my door while I'm hard at work sorting through my clothes. Natalie's party is in a week, and none of my clothes are cool enough. I might wind up wearing Annabelle's pink shirt and my own white shorts. Or maybe the black ones. I get tired just *thinking* about all the times in my life I'm going to have to find the right clothes for the right occasions. I'm so bad at it.

Mom knocks again. I toss the clothes onto my bed and open the door. She comes in wearing a sweat suit and resting

Sawyer on one hip. My mom is not the sweat suit type. "I'm taking an aerobics class at the community center," she announces. "Sawyer really likes the day care room there, so I'm going to take him with me. You okay staying home alone?"

I hadn't been home alone since "the incident," but I'm pretty sure I'd be okay this time. I'm about to say I'll be fine home alone, when I glance over at Bunny. His ears are pressed down against his head, and I'm pretty sure he just winked at me.

"I'll come with you," I say, hurrying to gather my books. "I'll just do homework on one of the couches there."

"You sure?" she asks.

I nod. Sawyer claps happily. It's nice to be wanted.

• • • • • • • • • • • •

Mom is late for her class, so I volunteer to take Sawyer into the playroom. It's full of kids around his age, some who have been on playdates at our house. I set him down, and he runs right over to the make-believe kitchen and starts frying a make-believe egg. If only he would eat a real one. On my way out the door, I notice a little dark-haired boy, around four or five, sitting by himself on a purple beanbag chair. His face has that crumpled about-to-cry look to it.

Both of the women running the playroom have their hands full with other kids, so I go over to him and sit down.

"Are you okay?" I ask.

He doesn't reply, just sniffles.

"Is your mom taking an exercise class? Mine is. I'm Sawyer's sister." I point to Sawyer, who has now moved on to washing pretend dishes. He's going to make some lucky girl a good husband someday.

I turn my attention back to the boy. He shakes his head. "I forgot my book."

"I hate when that happens," I tell him. "Do you want to pick out another one? They have a lot to choose from here."

He shakes his head. "I just want mine."

"Is it at home?"

He shakes his head. "My sister has it but she's busy."

"Where is she?"

"Dancing," he replies.

"Do you mean exercising?"

He shakes his head. "Dancing!"

"I'll go see if I can find her, okay?"

He nods, sinking lower into the beanbag.

I grab my book bag and head down the hall. All the other rooms are empty except for the thumping coming from the exercise room. No one practicing for a Bar Mitzvah, no one learning how to keep kids from cracking their heads open on a babysitting gig.

I backtrack into the main room and look around. A big sign catches my eye: REGIONAL AUDITIONS FOR THE BALLET SCHOOL OF AMERICA, UPSTAIRS IN MEETING ROOM B, PROMPTLY AT 11 A.M. So upstairs I go. When I get there, all I see is an empty table with some folders and pens on it. Then a bathroom door swings open and a tall girl in a leotard, who looks about sixteen, comes out. She slumps against the wall, head down. It would have been smart of me to actually get the *name* of the boy's sister.

"Um, is your brother in the playroom by any chance?"

Her head snaps up. Her eyes are red from crying. "Why? Is he okay?"

"He's fine," I assure her. "Something about you having his book?"

She looks puzzled, then says, "Oh, right," and reaches into a gym bag at her feet. She pulls out a well-worn copy of *Green Eggs and Ham*.

"Do you want me to bring it to him?"

She shakes her head. "I can do it. Looks like I'm done here anyway."

I glance at the empty desk and the door next to it. I can

hear classical music being played inside. "Did you try out already?"

She shakes her head and gestures to the clock above the table. "I got here late and the lady wouldn't let me in."

"But it's only five minutes after eleven now. How late could you have been?"

"It was one minute after when I got up here. I was only late because I had to take my brother downstairs first. But the lady at the desk said, 'Ballet is all about discipline and being on time is part of that,' and then she left."

"That's so unfair. I bet you wouldn't want to be a part of a program that treats you like that."

She shakes her head. "BSA is the best ballet school in this part of the country. If I got in, it would be a free ride to college. I really need that."

I glance at the clock. Six after now. "Where did the lady at the desk go?"

"I heard her tell someone she was going down for more coffee. Why?"

"Just go stand at the top of the stairs and warn me if you see her coming." Before she can ask anything else, I drop my bag on the ground and hurry over to the table. Little Emily St. Claire has taught me a trick or two. I climb up on the table, grab the plastic covering right off the clock, and turn the minute hand back to 10:58. Then

I replace the cover. The whole thing takes less than fifteen seconds.

Just as I hop down, the girl runs up from the top of the stairs and joins me in front of the table. She stares at me wordlessly. A few seconds later, a lady in a business suit appears, carrying a mug of coffee in one hand and a clipboard in another. She places them on the table, glances up at us, and says, "Yes?"

I step to the side as the girl clears her throat. "Um, I'd like to try out?"

The lady sighs. "Look, I don't make the rules, I just enforce them."

The girl points up at the clock. "But I'm not late. You must have read it wrong before. It's only 10:59."

The lady frowns, but turns to look. Then she does a double take and sighs. "Fine. Sign here." She pushes the clipboard at the girl, who eagerly signs it and passes it back. The lady hands her a folder and points her to the door. She picks up her gym bag, mouths "Thank you!" to me, and hurries inside the room.

"These auditions are only for older girls," the lady says curtly. "So if you were planning on trying out . . ."

I shake my head. "I wasn't. I wouldn't want to take another girl's spot." Honestly, sometimes I don't know where I come up with this stuff.

Back in the playroom, the little boy is sitting right where I left him. He snatches the book from my hands and then hides his face in it. I wave to Sawyer, who ignores me and keeps playing. Little kids are so fickle.

We have a vocabulary test on Monday, so that's the first thing I dive into when I get settled on one of the couches in the main room. I've only gotten down to the third word on the list, *coincidence*, when someone plops down next to me. I lay the list on my lap and turn to find Leo Fitzpatrick.

"Yo," he says.

"Yo to you."

"What brings you here on a fine Saturday morning?"

"Brother in the playroom, Mom exercising, potentially evil bunny at home. You?"

"I'm here to visit an old friend. I mean that literally, he's really old."

"I saw you and Amanda here once before."

He nods. "We come pretty regularly. These old guys are pretty cool. They have a lot of funny stories to tell."

"Speaking of telling stories . . ." I look around to make sure no one can hear us. "How about you tell me why you and Amanda suddenly became best friends again last year?"

He smiles and shakes his head. "You wouldn't believe me if I told you, which I can't."

"I might," I say hopefully.

He laughs and pushes himself off the couch. "Remember," he calls back to me as he walks away, "there are no such things as coincidences."

I glance down at my vocab list, and back up. "Wait, what do you mean?" But he's already joined a group of old guys playing cards and doesn't answer.

．　．　．　．　．　．　．　．　．　．　．

Lying in bed that night I keep thinking about what Leo said at the community center. Of course there are such things as coincidences. Like when I'm thinking about Annabelle and she calls me right then. Or when you happen to be at the right place at the right time, or the wrong place at the wrong time. I've had my share of both lately. So why would he say there isn't?

I toss and turn for a while and am no closer to figuring out what he meant by the time I fall asleep. This time, my nightmare is the worst I've ever had. I dream that someone is holding a pillow over my face and pressing down on it. I'm kicking and swinging my arms, but nothing helps. I awake with a start, so relieved that it was just a dream that I want to weep with joy.

But like last time, I quickly realize that I can't catch my breath! I'm really suffocating! This is different from the other dream. Worse, if that's possible. I can't even make a gasping noise because I can't get any air through my mouth or nose. My eyes fly open in panic, but this time I don't see a glowing red pair of eyes staring back at me.

I can't see anything at all.

Chapter Fifteen

I plop the cage on the counter. "This rabbit tried to kill me. I would like to return him."

The pet store manager nods. "Figured it was just a matter of time. Didn't earn that name for nothing."

"Kyle R? Isn't he just named after someone named Kyle?"

He laughs. "Say his name three times fast."

"Huh?"

"Just do it."

"KyleR, KyleR, KyleR." I step back from the counter. *"Killer?"*

He nods. "That's right."

"So you sold me a *killer rabbit*?"

"He's just a little feisty, is all."

"*Feisty?* Last night I woke up with him lying on my *face*. I couldn't breathe!"

He picks up the cage and puts it behind the desk. "You really shouldn't let a rabbit sleep with you."

"I didn't! He was locked in his cage. With extra tape around the door!"

The man looks skeptical, but opens the cash register and hands me forty dollars. "This oughta cover it. And how about I throw in a goldfish? Not likely to kill you."

Before I can tell him not to bother, he's already swishing a net around the closest fish tank. Mom and Sawyer arrive while he's scooping a goldfish into a plastic bag. They're each nibbling a hot pretzel. Since hot pretzels are pretty much the only thing I eat in the cafeteria every day, I turn it down when offered. I'm glad to see Sawyer is branching out, though.

"I really don't need one," I tell the manager when he goes to hand me the fish.

"Goldfish!" Sawyer says, jumping up and snatching it. Good thing the knot in the bag is tight.

"You're sure you want to do this, Rory?" Mom asks. "You loved that fluffy little guy."

I take a last look at Bunny. His cute orange ears are still cute. His soft white fur is still soft. And his adorable little wiggling nose is still adorable. But inside his bunny chest lies a heart of stone.

"I'm sure. Let's go."

She puts her arm around me, and I put mine around Sawyer. The three of us walk out of the store, and right smack into Alexa, Natalie, Mena, Heather, and Jess. And I mean *right smack into them*, in that way that makes glasses slide down your nose and people holding bags drop them. And these girls were holding a lot of bags. I fix my glasses and see that they've been busy shopping in at least five different clothing stores, along with a bunch of makeup and accessories shops. Sawyer's goldfish bag had also gone flying, but luckily it landed at Mom's feet and didn't break. As soon as the girls sort out whose bag is whose, they focus their attention to me. I brace for the worst.

"Aren't you the girl who always wears that weird hat?" Mena asks.

I glance at Mom and nod reluctantly. "Um, I don't really need it anymore."

"That's good to hear, Rory," Natalie says, adjusting the pocketbook on her shoulder. "I was afraid you were going to wear it to my party."

"So you *are* going to Natalie's party!" Alexa exclaims. "Interesting!"

I know she's thinking about our IM, the one she thought she was having with Boy Rory. I wonder if they ever got that sorted out.

Alexa notices Sawyer. "Hey, I recognize you! You have more clothes on now, though!"

The other girls laugh.

"We've got to get going, Rory," Mom says, steering me and Sawyer away. "You girls have a lovely day."

They giggle and head toward the food court.

We don't speak the whole way out to the car. Well, except for Sawyer, who has been bellowing "Twinkle, Twinkle, Little Star" at the top of his lungs ever since the collision. I climb in and stare straight ahead. Mom puts Sawyer into his car seat and joins me up front. She doesn't start the car, though. Instead, she clears her throat and asks, "How's your list coming?"

I look over, surprised. She's never really acknowledged my list before. "Only three things left. Getting contact lenses, going to Natalie's party, and riding the upside-down roller coaster."

"Then what are we waiting for?" She starts the car and backs out of the spot. "Let's go get those lenses."

"It's a Sunday, Mom. The eye doctor's closed."

She slows down. "Oh, right. Well, I'll pick you up after school tomorrow, and we'll go then."

I watch her out of the corner of my eye. "You have a coupon, don't you?"

"Maybe."

The whole way home I think about how at least *one* of my attempts to look better for the party is actually going to happen. I won't have makeup, or earrings, or hair-free legs, but at least I won't have glasses, either.

. . . .

The next day, since we made such a last minute appointment, we're told we'll have to wait a little while. Sawyer isn't great in waiting rooms. He likes to climb over all the chairs — even if other people are sitting in them. Once Mom got caught up reading a copy of *People* magazine, and Sawyer started going through a lady's purse on the chair next to them. The lady didn't think it was very funny and threatened to press charges.

Luckily for everyone, this office building has a built-in babysitting room. Anyone visiting any of the doctors in the whole building can bring their kids to this room for only a dollar an hour. We drop Sawyer off, and he happily joins the other kids to watch *The Lion King*.

Back in the waiting room, I keep busy by looking through the contact lenses brochures. "Hey, Mom, look." I hold up the brochure. She keeps reading her magazine. Undaunted, I ask, "Did you know you can get contacts that look like cat's eyes? Or with little smiley faces in the middle?"

She flips her page. "You're not getting those."

I lean back in my seat. "I know. I was just saying."

After a few more minutes we get called into Dr. Levinson's office. She's been my eye doctor since I failed the vision test at school when I was six. She's always been very nice to me, which helps when you're the only first grader who has to wear glasses.

"So you're finally ready to try contacts?" she asks.

"I've been ready," I reply. "It was my mother who wasn't ready."

"Hey, we're here now, aren't we?" Mom says.

Dr. Levinson checks something in my file, and says, "Usually we need to do a full checkup before fitting you for contacts, but your annual checkup was just a few months ago, so we can use that prescription."

This is great news, because it means I won't have to deal with that machine that blows a puff of air into your eye. I always dread that part.

"All we need to do is measure the curvature of your corneas to make sure we fit you with the right size," she says. "I should warn you, contact lenses are a big commitment. You have to apply them very carefully, and then clean and change them as often as the type you choose requires. Otherwise, you can damage your eyes, and even permanently warp your cornea. It's a big responsibility. I always tell parents to ask themselves how well their child follows through with their homework, or how well they take care of the family pet. Those are good indicators of how well they'll do with contacts."

Mom frowns. "Rory *did* just return her pet rabbit after less than two weeks. . . ."

I whirl to face her. "He tried to kill me!"

She shrugs. "Nevertheless."

Figures Mom wouldn't let this be easy.

Dr. Levinson raises her eyebrows, but doesn't pry. "You're probably aware that there are many different types of lenses. For kids your age, I'm a fan of the disposable soft lenses. They're very comfortable, and easier for the eye to adapt to than the hard lenses."

I hold up the brochure. "What about the ones you don't have to take out for thirty days? Those sounded good."

She shakes her head. "I don't recommend those for my younger patients. The chance for a negative reaction is too great."

I let the brochure drop onto the desk. Well, that solves that! I've had enough negative reactions recently to last a lifetime.

Dr. Levinson pushes back her chair. "The first step is to make sure you feel comfortable inserting and removing the lenses. No sense going further before then." She leads us over to a little nook with different-sized mirrors, bottles of contact solution, and boxes of different lenses. "Sarah, our contact lens technician, will help you from here. Let me know if you have any questions."

Sarah comes over a few minutes later with a tray. On the tray are little plastic cups with lenses floating in what looks like water, but Sarah says it's called saline solution.

"We like to use colored contacts for this part," she explains, "so when the iris turns color, you'll know you got the lens in the right place."

We all wash our hands in preparation. First she shows me how to put them in by demonstrating on herself. She lifts the lens out of the solution by touching it with the pad of her middle finger, holds her eye open with the other hand, looks down, pops the lens in, then lifts her eye and blinks it into place. Her blue eye is now brown! Then to remove it, she looks up, pushes the lens down with her fingertip, grasps the sides with her thumb and forefinger, and pinches it out. And that's it! Looks so simple!

But apparently it only *looks* simple. When I try to pick up my own lens, I can't even get it to stick on my fingertip. It goes downhill from there. Once I manage to get it out of the solution, I keep dropping it on the floor and we have to start over with another lens. Mom is no help because the thought of someone touching their eye makes her squeamish. After another ten minutes, I'm able to keep the lens balanced on my finger long enough to bring it toward my eye, but then I'm incapable of bringing the lens any closer than an inch. I try holding my eye open like Sarah had done, but it keeps blinking itself closed again as soon as my finger approaches. My eye has a mind of its own.

Another patient comes and goes. Mom abandons me to watch the movie with Sawyer. Dr. Levinson walks over, assesses the situation, and suggests she place the lens in my eye for me. That way at least I'll get the feel of it. I agree. She puts on a rubber glove, picks the lens up on her finger and leans toward me. I lean away. I can't help it, honestly.

She smiles patiently. "Rory, if you don't want to do this, you don't have to."

"I really do want to," I promise. "Let's try again."

She leans in. I lean out. She tries again. Same thing. She suggests we try it lying down on the dentistlike chair in the examination room. I think that's a good idea. Nowhere for me to back up. I lie down and she leans over me, holds my right eye firmly open, and before I have a chance to think (or blink), she pops it in. I sit up, my eye watering.

She hands me a mirror. "Take a look."

I blink away the tears. It feels weird against my eyelid. Not bad, just like I know something's in there. I look in the mirror. "I have one brown eye!" I close my eye and touch my finger gently on the outside of the lid to see if I can feel it. I can. "It feels a little weird, though."

"This particular lens is larger than what you'll wind up with. When we measure your curvature we'll know better. You ready to try taking it out now?"

I nod. She leads me back to the desk and hands me over to Sarah. I cover my green eye with my hand. I look like a totally different person with brown eyes. Or brown *eye*, to be precise.

Sarah goes over the removal process again, and I listen carefully. But when it comes time to do it . . . surprise, surprise . . . I can't. Time passes. Sarah checks her watch. Mom comes in to say that Sawyer needs to nap or even singing lion cubs won't be able to calm him. She's not impressed with my brown eye.

"Okay, okay," I say, taking a deep breath. "I can do this." Following Sarah's example, I open my eye wide, and look up. Then I force myself to reach in and grab it. As I'm grabbing, a few things happen. Sarah says, "Be sure to push it down off your cornea first, into the white area." Mom comes back in and says, "Ack, can't look," and the next thing I know, I feel a searing pain, like a paper cut, but in my eye. Mom and Sarah carry me back into the exam room and lay me down. The receptionist is entertaining Sawyer, who was very upset when he heard me scream and saw me clutch at my eye.

"What you have is a mild corneal abrasion," Dr. Levinson says when I finally take my hand away from my eye so she can examine it with a magnifying glass. It hurts every time I blink and my eye is tearing like crazy from the bright light. "This can happen if you grasp the lens with your fingernail instead of the soft part of your finger," she says. "Also, you'll want to avoid trying to take it out directly over the cornea."

I really had been trying to follow the directions. I don't know what went wrong. It all happened so fast.

"So now what?" Mom says, pacing in the small office.

"Mild abrasions like this to the outer layer of the cornea regenerate rapidly, usually within forty-eight hours. The discomfort you're feeling is from the eyelid rubbing against the uneven cornea."

It's a little more than discomfort, but I don't want Mom to get even more worked up, so I let it pass.

"We have two options," Dr. Levinson says. "We can patch the eye, which would entail putting in a drop of antibiotic ointment and taping the eye closed. Or what we do more often now is to put in an antibiotic drop, and then place a disposable extended-wear contact lens over it to protect it from the eyelid. Either way, you'll likely want to wear a patch over the eye because it will be light sensitive and teary while it heals, and we don't want you rubbing it. Plus, there'll be some oozing."

"Did you say a *patch*?" I ask. "Like a pirate?"

"I'm afraid so," she says. "But it's only for two days or so. You could look at it like an extended Halloween!"

I groan.

"Which option do you think you'd like?" she asks gently.

The idea of having another lens stuck in my eye isn't very appealing, but having my eye taped shut is definitely too creepy. "I'll go with the lens."

She nods. "Good. Then let's get started. You can stay there on the couch."

My phone rings a few times as I wait for her to return, but I don't bother to see who it is. Can someone text with only one eye? I'm not sure.

Once the ointment is in and the lens placed on top of it, it doesn't hurt anymore when I blink. The patch is as bad as I feared. Black, with a thin elastic band that goes around my head to hold it on. At least I won't have to look at my eye oozing.

Mom guides me out to the waiting room where Sawyer

is playing cards with the receptionist. I can't see any way to hide the patch from him, so I don't even bother. He takes one look at me, and instead of bursting into tears like I expected, he starts laughing and chants, "Rory is a pirate! Rory is a pirate!" He doesn't stop all the way out to the car.

I think I'd prefer the crying.

When we stop at the one light in downtown Willow Falls, I ask Mom if I can stay home from school tomorrow. Dr. Levinson has to check my eye sometime tomorrow anyway. Usually I have to be at death's door before Mom lets me stay home, but she must be taking pity on me because she says yes. I watch out the window with my one good eye, and think about how if this happened to Jake, he and his patch would be plastered all over the teen magazines and the tabloids. Although he'd probably start a new trend or something. At least my mistakes don't follow me outside of Willow Falls. That's something to be grateful for.

Mom must have called Dad while I was being patched by the doctor, because when I walk in the door, all he says is, "Annabelle called. She said you didn't answer your cell."

I don't respond.

"Um, do you want to call her back?" He holds out the cordless phone.

I don't take it.

"Sooo . . . how was school today?"

"Dad! I'm wearing a patch! I look like a pirate! You can't pretend not to notice!"

He shrugs. "What patch?"

"UGH!" I try to run upstairs, but running with only one eye is next to impossible. Dr. Levinson says I won't have "depth perception" as long as the patch is on, and she's right. I can hardly tell if my feet are going to land on the right steps.

"Let me help you," Dad says, climbing up to take my arm.

"Thought you didn't see anything," I mumble.

"Can't a dad just help his beautiful, one-eyed daughter up the stairs?"

I stop climbing. "Too soon for jokes, Dad."

"You sure?"

"Positive."

"Aye aye, matey."

"Dad!"

"Sorry, honey."

"No more pirate talk!"

"Okay. Can we talk about the bunny?"

"No!"

He stays quiet the rest of the way upstairs, which I'm thankful for. My bedroom feels empty without Bunny, and I worry for a second that I did the wrong thing by returning him. Then I remember the near-death experience and decide that I did what I had to do, for my own safety and that of my loved ones. I mean, what if he hopped his way into Sawyer's room and went after him next? Who knows what he had planned in his devious little mind.

Dad leads me to my desk chair and asks if I'm going to be okay. I nod. "I only have to wear this for two days."

"Wear what?"

I throw a shoe at him.

He holds up his hands in surrender and backs out of my room. My phone keeps buzzing to alert me that I have voice mails. Instead of playing them, I just call Annabelle.

"Finally!" she says, answering on the first ring. "I've been calling you all day!"

"Why?"

"We've got a really early morning shoot tomorrow! It's a classroom scene. That means lots of close-ups! I wanted to make sure you got Brenda's call this time."

I close my eyes and lean my head back on my chair. "I'm not going to school tomorrow."

"What? Why? Are you sick?"

"Not exactly."

"But you can't skip the filming, or they'll drop you."

"Maybe they won't notice."

"They'll notice if you don't sign in."

"Maybe Boy Rory can sign in twice!" I suggest.

"But don't you want the money?"

"Well, I don't have Bunny anymore anyway, so I don't need it as much."

"But you're gonna get a new pet, right? One that doesn't lie in its cage all day plotting against you?"

"I don't know. I'm not sure." I'm not sure about a lot of things anymore, but I don't say that.

"Your dad said you were getting contacts today. Did you get them?"

I shift in my chair. "Not exactly."

"Why not?"

I pause. "I don't want to talk about it."

"If you quit the movie, then I'm quitting. It's no fun without you."

"You can't quit."

"Then you have to be there tomorrow."

I sigh. "Maybe."

"Great!" she squeals. "See you bright and early!"

I rest my forehead on my desk as dramatically as I can, only to lift it right back up because the pressure hurts my eye. Might as well check my e-mail. The newest one is from Dad, of all people. I don't think he's ever e-mailed me before. He sent it only two minutes ago. I click to open it.

Hi, Honey. I know you're feeling blue, but I just wanted to share an old saying with you: In the land of the blind, the one-eyed man is king. Or in your case, queen. Your mom and I love you very much and are very proud of you. Do you want to come down for dinner? Chocolate chip pancakes . . . Love always, Dad.

Imagine! Bribing me with chocolate chip pancakes, as though it were that easy to cheer me up! And I'm not sure what they have to be proud of. I mess everything up.

Although . . . eating chocolate chip pancakes is certainly better than *not* eating chocolate chip pancakes. I push back my desk chair. I guess it *is* that easy!

• • • • • • • • • • •

Mom drops me off at school while the sun is only barely peeking over the horizon. She agrees to come back to pick me up after dropping Sawyer at preschool. We should be done shooting by then. Stepping very carefully, I make my way into the school and down the hall to the room number Brenda had left in her message. The hall outside is set up with the lights, too, which means a hallway scene as well as a classroom scene. Keeping my head down, I step around the equipment in the hall, take a deep breath, and enter the classroom. Of course the first person to notice me is the director.

"What do you think we're shooting here, *Pirates of the Caribbean*? Do you see Johnny Depp anywhere?"

I lower my eyes and shake my head.

"Then what's with the patch?"

The few other extras who have arrived so far stop what they're doing and listen. I mutter something about a contact lens accident.

"This I've got to see!" a voice from behind me says. I turn to face Jake, silently cursing Annabelle for making me come this morning. She's not even here yet to rescue me.

He takes one look at my face and bursts out laughing. He literally holds his stomach and bends forward. He's laughing *that* hard.

"Okay, okay," I say, crossing my arms. "It's not THAT funny!"

"Yes," he gasps. "It is!"

"You're sitting this one out," the director barks.

"Wait," Brenda says, joining us. "I have an idea."

She leads the director away by the elbow, while Jake, bent over, continues to shake with laughter. This is how Annabelle finds us when she finally walks in.

"It's never boring being your best friend," she says. "Just when I think I've seen it all, you outdo yourself."

Brenda comes back and asks, "Would you be able to take the patch off and walk a few feet?"

Unsure where this is going, I say, "I guess so."

Ten minutes later, the camera rolling, we film our hall scene. The camera is focused on me (known in the scene as "girl with phone") as I walk down the crowded hallway, pretending to text on my phone. The view is from my right side, so you can't see that my left eye is red and leaky. Suddenly Jake flings open his locker, and since my character is not looking where she's going, it hits me right in the face. (In reality, he's supposed to stop the locker right before it hits me, but it kind of hits me anyway.) "Are you all right?" he asks in a voice skilled at squeezing a lot of emotion out of a few words. He bends over me in concern as I cover my eye with my hands as though it hadn't already been injured. The director yells, "Cut!" and they move the cameras to the other side. After a few lighting adjustments, the PA hands me my patch, and the director yells, "Action!" I walk down the hallway again, this time with the patch over my eye. As I pass Jake at his locker, he exclaims, "There goes the latest victim of the worst epidemic in our schools today — Walking While Texting!"

The crew and the other extras all clap when we're done, and I know without looking that my face is bright red. The best part was how Madison had to stand on the side while we filmed it. The second-best part was getting paid fifty dollars. Fifty dollars! That's more money than I've ever gotten at one time in my entire life.

All the same, I still leave with Mom afterward. Being a "cautionary tale" for the movie was one thing, but I have no need to hear "Ahoy, matey!" and "Yo-ho-ho, shiver me timbers" from the kids at school all day. I could get *that* at home.

Which, of course, I do.

Chapter Sixteen

Now that I'm allowed to pick out my own clothes and have fifty dollars from my big movie scene burning a hole in my pocket, Mom agrees to take me shopping after school on Friday. I suggest one of the small shops in the center of town. I'm taking a break from the mall. I'm afraid Bunny is sitting in his cage at the pet store, plotting his revenge.

Mom is very well behaved, and sits patiently in the dressing room while I try on a zillion outfits, never admitting if she likes them or not. But since I've known her for twelve years, it's pretty easy to tell by the eye rolls, tight mouth, raised brows, imperceptible nods, or slight upturn of lips.

The day of the party is sunny and warm, just like I knew it would be when I imagined it. "You sure it looks okay?" I ask Mom for the tenth time, turning from side to side in front of her full-length mirror.

"Yes!" she replies, also for the tenth time. I had finally left the store with a brown and white sundress and brown sandals, but now that it's time to actually wear the outfit, I wonder if it was the right choice. Regular brown Band-Aids cover my still-pretty-scabby legs, and the patch was retired a few days ago, but I still feel like I'm not ready. And Annabelle's mom is coming to pick me up any minute, which isn't helping my anxiety level.

"Here," Mom says, handing me a tube of pink lip gloss. "This only contains artificial chemicals. None of that good, all-natural stuff like trees or berries."

"Cool, thanks!" I say, rolling it on.

"And one more thing." She reaches into her pocket and pulls out a small silk pouch. She opens the drawstring and Grandma's earrings spill out onto her palm.

"But I can't wear those," I say, confused.

"Yes, you can." To my surprise, she leans over and clips one on each ear. They pinch a tiny bit, especially on the previously pierced ear, but I'll get used to it. I can't believe she had them made into clip-ons without telling me. "Check them out," she says, facing me toward the mirror.

"Wow. I look good!" I still look twelve, but now I look more like what I picture in my head a twelve-year-old should look like. Or maybe I look extra-good because noth-ing is currently swollen, bleeding, leaking pus, or covered with a patch.

"You have your cell?" she asks, back to business.

"Check."

"And extra money?"

"Check."

"And your house key in case we're not home when you get back?"

"Check."

"And Natalie's gift?"

"Yup." It had taken me a while to figure out what to get her. But then I found that book I had bought at the mall the day of the unfortunate incident with the makeup, and remembered that Natalie had done a book report in fourth grade on the first book in the series and had loved it, too. So I wrapped up my copy of the sequel and added a really cool flashlight that I bought at the drugstore, because it's really a flashlight-under-the-covers type of read.

Mom stands back to admire me and nods, satisfied. "Well, then, I guess you're all set for your first boy-girl party."

"It's the last thing on my list," I inform her. "Well, except for the upside-down roller coaster. But that's on the Small Things list."

"Small, but still very important and worthwhile," Mom says, winking.

So she HAS been reading my chart!

"You know," she says, sitting down on her bed, "the Willow Falls carnival is in town for a few more days. I promised Sawyer cotton candy, and at this point, if he says he'll eat anything other than pizza and the occasional hot pretzel, I'm inclined to let him. We could go after dinner, if you like. You should be home from the party by then."

"That would be great! Thanks." I have to admit, Mom has really been supportive of my whole list thing, even though she tried to fight it in the beginning.

She pops up off the bed. "Well, I hope this party is everything you hope it will be, and more."

The car honking in the driveway spares me from having to think too deeply about that.

Natalie lives on the other side of town in this strange kind of neighborhood. One half of the street has these small or medium-sized houses like the one where Mom took Sawyer for his playdate a few weeks ago. Then across the street are these new, huge houses with big lawns and swimming pools. Natalie's house is one of the new, huge ones. I've been there a few times over the years, mostly when we were younger and Natalie's and Annabelle's families used to do more things together. They have a heart-shaped pool with its own pool house next to it, where you can get changed and stuff. The pool house is almost as big as some of the houses down the street!

Natalie's mom hugs us hello at the front door and takes our gifts. She tells us the party is in the backyard, which we could already tell since the whole back of the house is glass and we can see right through it. I follow Annabelle through the house and out the back door.

Balloons are strung on the backs of plastic chairs, and streamers hang suspended in the trees. Her dad and uncle are sizzling burgers on a huge barbecue grill, and her older brother and his friends are practicing with their band in the corner of the yard. The pool is crystal clear, with lights in it that keep changing the color of the water from blue to red to green and back again.

Out of the corner of my mouth, I ask Annabelle if we were supposed to bring bathing suits. She shakes her head. This is good news, because wearing my bathing suit in front of my classmates is not something I'm looking forward to doing anytime soon.

We stand on the grass off to the side of the main action, which is where Annabelle told Sari in a text that we would meet her. The grass tickles my ankles in a way that's both pleasant and really annoying.

I'm not sure what to do with my hands, so I keep playing with the strap of the little pocketbook Mom lent me.

"I love your earrings!" Sari gushes as she runs up to us. "You guys look great!" She's saying it to both of us, but is looking at me. Annabelle always looks great, so it sort of goes without saying in her case.

"Thanks," I reply. I won't tell her how many hours it took to find the dress. Sari's wearing a miniskirt and two tanks layered on top of each other, and I'm sure she picked it out of her closet in two seconds. Annabelle's wearing the same outfit she lent me for the dance scene. But on her the skirt is the right length.

People keep streaming in, and soon the backyard is full of kids. I recognize all of them from school, except a few of Natalie's friends from camp. They cling together; laughing about the time they all snuck out of the bunk one night and got poison ivy. This doesn't sound very funny to me, but I've never been to camp so maybe it is. Natalie huddles with the gymnastics crowd on lawn chairs by the pool, and all the boys push and shove one another in that way that boys do when they don't know what else to do.

Sari and Annabelle have launched into a conversation about whether you're supposed to match your nail polish to your clothes or your skin tone, and I know from years of experience that the conversation will move from nails to hair, makeup, and the hair and makeup of those around us. Deciding that the spiky grass has progressed from half annoying to fully annoying, I step a few feet away and sit down on one of the plastic folding chairs set up on the lawn. I curl my legs underneath me (careful not to scrape against the still tender areas), and think about the fact that after tonight, I'll have crossed everything off my list. It's definitely been the craziest few weeks of my entire life. I haven't even had a chance to digest it all and to sort out how I feel about everything.

I look out over the party scene, thinking how if it were being filmed for the movie, it would look exactly like this. Groups of friends keeping close together, balloons swaying in the breeze, glasses of soda and juice being passed around. There's also a ripple of excitement underneath, because I know everyone's waiting for Natalie's parents to go inside. But behind all that, I can see little things, like that Boy Rory keeps checking his watch, or that one of Natalie's camp friends is hanging a half-step back from the group and her smile seems forced.

Annabelle glances back over at me and fake-talks, "Everything okay?"

I nod, and she turns back to her conversation. I don't mind sitting here alone. It feels like how it used to, back when I didn't have some sort of disfigurement that made everyone notice me. Then suddenly I'm not alone. Amanda Ellerby has sat down in the chair next to me.

She tucks her feet under her like mine are, and balances a cup of bright orange soda on her leg. "So . . . what was it like getting hit in the head with a locker by Jake Harrison?"

I laugh. "Pretty much how you'd expect."

"I wish filming wasn't ending next week."

"Me too."

Amanda lifts her cup and takes a long drink. I think I'm supposed to keep the conversation going, but I'm not sure how. I'm gearing up to ask a question about her drum playing, when she blurts out, "Leo and I are having our birthday party two weeks from Saturday. Can you come?"

After my initial surprise, I say, "Sure, that sounds great."

"Cool. It's going to be really small. Wear gardening clothes."

"Gardening clothes?"

She nods. "We're going to be planting seeds out by where old Apple Grove used to be."

"That's, um, *different*."

"Yeah, we thought it would be fun to try to grow apple trees again in Willow Falls."

"And Leo's okay without having a hypnotist and a giant iguana?" Even though I hadn't gone to his party last year (the whole boy-girl thing), everyone knew about it.

Amanda laughs. "He's handling the disappointment pretty well."

The band starts playing and some of the girls get up to dance. I watch the crowd; Amanda sips her drink. She must be really thirsty. "So . . . whatcha looking at?" she asks casually. Almost *too* casually. I'm suddenly on the alert.

"Is there something I *should* be looking at?"

"I don't know. That's sort of your thing, ya know?"

This girl isn't making much sense. "What's my thing?"

"You know, how you see things."

"I'm not sure what you mean. I was just looking at everyone." I gesture at the crowd.

She shakes her head. "No. Other people *look*. You *see*. Looking isn't the same as seeing." And with that completely bizarre statement, she gets up and leaves. My mouth falls open a little at the abruptness of it all.

"What was that all about?" Annabelle asks, sitting in the now-empty chair.

I shake my head. "It's weird. It's like Amanda and Leo know something about me that I don't even know."

We watch as Amanda joins Leo and some of his guy friends on line for burgers. "Like what?" Annabelle asks.

"I'm not sure. But they've been saying strange things to me ever since I bought lunch that first day in the cafeteria."

She shrugs. "Why don't you ask them?"

"I don't think it would do any good."

"Someday we've gotta find out what happened with them last year." She takes my arm and tugs. "But right now I'm really hungry so let's get some food before it's all gone." While we wait on the long line, Annabelle says something about how Natalie's parents are going to leave right after they finish feeding us, and how after that everyone's going into the pool house. I'm only half listening though, because Amanda's words are still circling around my mind. They seem almost familiar, somehow, like I've heard them — or something like them — before. Or maybe I'm just imagining things. After the crazy events of the last few weeks, anything's possible.

"Rory, are you listening to me?" Annabelle asks, hands on her hips.

"What? Yes, I'm listening. Parents. Food. Pool house. Got it."

"I asked you who you hope you get!"

I do my best to focus. "Who do I hope I get for what?" Why is no one making sense today?

We're almost at the front of the line now. Keeping one eye on Natalie's dad, Annabelle leans over and whispers, "For the game!"

"What game?"

Burgers and chips are now being dropped on our plates, and sodas pressed into our hands. Annabelle doesn't answer until we're out of earshot of any adults. "The kissing games in the pool house!"

My heart quickens. Kissing games? How did I miss that? "I . . . I don't know." Usually when faced with doing something new, I'd always assumed I wasn't allowed to do it, due to the whole strictest-parents-in-the-world thing. My hand automatically moves toward my cell phone, but I pull it back. I don't need to ask anyone. I'm allowed to be at boy-girl parties, so that means I'm allowed to do what everyone else is doing.

We join Sari at a table full of kids, all scarfing down their food as fast as they can. Every few seconds someone checks the movements of the adults out of the corners of their eyes. Cupcakes are handed out, and Natalie blows out her candle so fast I almost didn't get to make a wish on it. Almost.

Soon enough, her parents are gone. Not an uncle or aunt in sight. I glance over at Natalie's brother's band, but they're so into their playing that they probably wouldn't notice if a spaceship landed and abducted all of us.

One by one, kids start making their way into the pool house. I hear Ruby say, "Oh, I think I left my bathing suit here last week. Do you want to help me check?" and all the other gymnastics girls run in after her, giggling. Then one of the boys says, "Hey, I think they've got a soccer ball in there that we can kick around." Six guys push and shove to get inside first.

"C'mon," Annabelle says, pulling me by the arm. She catches the door before it closes and pushes me through it. All of the shades in the large, square-shaped room have been pulled down, which makes it seem like it's nighttime in the middle of the day.

"I'll be right back," I tell Annabelle, pushing gently through the crowd before she has a chance to stop me. The bathroom is attached to the main room through a small hall. I lock the door behind me and turn on the light. The toilet itself is behind its own door, so someone could change into their bathing suit in private, if they liked. I go into the stall and sit down on the closed toilet seat.

For lack of anything better to do, I start taking things out of my purse. First, the lip gloss. Might as well put more on, since I'm sure mine wore off when I ate. After that, I lift out my house key and turn it over a few times. I wonder what my family's doing at home. I heard Dad say something about building a fort for Sawyer out of old boxes and blankets. I like forts. When I was younger, Dad used to build them with me, and then we'd crawl inside and read comics with our flashlights. I suddenly worry that Natalie won't like my gift. She probably doesn't play in many forts these days. I put the key back into the purse and pull out my cell phone. As always, the weight of it in my hand makes me happy. I'm also very proud of myself that I haven't lost it since that first day. My fingers move toward the numbers. My hand seems to know I'm about to call Mom even before my brain does.

I've only gotten to the first three numbers when I hear voices outside the door. I freeze as the outside knob to the bathroom jiggles. "It's locked," a girl's voice says, sounding disappointed. I let out my breath, relieved I'd remembered to lock it. More jiggling. "Wait," the girl says, pushing against it, "I think it's just stuck." And to my horror, the door bangs open! I instantly pull my legs up onto the seat. This is getting to be a pattern. Nothing good came out of it last time, and I'm not expecting a happy ending this time, either.

The girl, giggling, says, "C'mon, we only have five minutes

before it's someone else's turn." I know I recognize her voice, but I can't think straight enough to place it.

My eyes widen when a boy's voice replies, "Okay, okay," and he pushes the door closed behind him.

"So . . ." the girl says, "how come you're never online anymore? I haven't seen your screen name pop up since our IM that time, like, weeks ago."

"What IM?"

Omigod. It's Alexa and Boy Rory! And of course now the soda is telling me I really *do* need to use the bathroom. I scrunch into an even smaller ball, if that's possible.

"Sure we did," Alexa says. "We even talked about this party."

"Sorry," he says. "Just didn't happen."

I'd love to peek through the wooden slats to see Alexa's expression right now, but I don't dare.

After a pause she says, "Well, we only have two minutes left. Are we gonna kiss or what?"

"Why not?" Boy Rory replies.

I roll my eyes. *How romantic.* For the next two minutes I squeeze my eyes closed and cover my ears with my hands, one of which is still grasping my phone. I'd hum to block out the noise even more, but can't risk detection.

After the longest 120 seconds in human history, the door opens and they leave. I scramble out of the stall and lock the main door. This time I notice one of those chain locks on the top, which must be there because the one on the knob doesn't work. I quickly latch the chain and hurry back to the stall. Right as I turn around to flush, the knob jiggles, no doubt with the next happy couple. "Just a minute," I call out, heart pounding. I try to do everything at once — flush, stick my phone back in my purse, put my purse back on my arm, straighten my dress. I hear the *plop* before I see it. Wincing and praying, I turn around and peek in the toilet. My worst fear is confirmed. There, on the bottom of the bowl, lies my cell phone. With only a second's hesitation, I reach in, grab it, wrap it in toilet paper, and stuff it in my purse. Then I let myself out of the stall and wash my hands really, really well.

"Hurry up in there!" a boy's voice says, knocking on the door. "We don't have all day!"

I don't bother to reply, just push my way out, without even bothering to see who it is. Then an arm grabs me and I stop and turn. Annabelle!

"Hey!" she says. "Are you okay? You've been gone forever!"

"Actually, I don't feel great. I think I'm going to call my mom to pick me up."

I glance over to see that the boy who was knocking before is Leo's friend Vinnie, who is an extra with us. I'd seen him and Annabelle talking a few times, but she never mentioned that she liked him or anything.

"Are you sure?" she asks. Then she glances at Vinnie, who is pointing to his watch and tapping his foot. "Do you mind if I stay?"

"No, you totally should. I'll call you later."

"Okay," she says, reaching out to hug me. "Feel better." Vinnie holds the door open for Annabelle to enter first, then he closes it behind them with a wave.

Leaning against the wall, I open my purse and unwrap the wet toilet paper until I reach the phone. Hoping against hope, I press some buttons. No beeps. No lights flash on the screen. Nothing. This is even *worse* than a fine kettle of fish. Not that I actually know what a kettle of fish *is*.

I drop the phone in my purse, and head back into the main pool house. The group has thinned. I easily slip out the front door and have to blink against the brightness. The band is still playing, but now it's not really music, it's more like noise, like they're all playing their instruments at once. Sari is sitting on a slope of grass talking to some kids from our gym class, although I'm not sure how they can hear one another over the band. When I approach, Sari looks up and asks, "Is it our turn yet?" and I realize the people outside are just waiting to be the people *inside*. I shake my head and ask to borrow her phone. She digs it out of her pocket and hands it to me.

"What happened to yours?"

"I'd rather not say."

She shrugs happily and returns to the group. I walk to a relatively quiet corner of the yard and call Mom.

"Sari?" she says. "What's wrong? Where's Rory?"

"It's me, Mom. I'm just using Sari's phone."

"Oh, phew, okay. Wait, what's wrong with your own phone?"

I sigh. "I'd rather not say."

"Why are you calling? The party's not over yet, is it?"

"Not exactly . . . I was just thinking maybe you could pick me up a little early?"

She doesn't answer, and for a second I worry we lost the connection. Then she says, "It'll take me at least twenty minutes to get there. Is that okay?"

"No problem."

"Do you want me to come inside?"

I shake my head, then feel stupid since obviously she can't see me. "No, no, I'll wait out front."

"Okay."

I give Sari her phone back, and tell her the same story I told Annabelle. She raises an eyebrow, but doesn't question me. I walk around to the front of the house, sit down on the tall curb, and tuck my dress around my legs.

The band must be taking a break because I can't hear them anymore. In fact, it's very quiet except for some far-away dog barking. Not a single car goes by in my first minute out here. I shift my weight a bit. It feels strange to be sitting alone in an unfamiliar neighborhood. All the houses suddenly look weird, like no one lives in any of them and I'm the only person on the planet. Well, the only person except for Jason from *Friday the 13th*, who no doubt is lurking behind a nearby tree. I probably shouldn't have watched that movie.

A dog barks, and I jump right off the curb and scramble onto the lawn. A big yellow dog lumbers down the street toward me, followed by a tall girl in shorts and a T-shirt, waving a leash. "Come back here, Bandit! Bad dog!"

Bandit is only a few feet away from me now. He looks happy enough, tail wagging and ears up, but I'm not taking any chances. Keeping my eye on him, I back up farther. He reaches the curb and sniffs. "Wait a minute, I know you," I tell him. "You're that dog I caught!"

"Hey, it's you!" the girl says, coming up behind the dog and snapping the leash on his collar.

I look up at her face. It's the girl from the ballet auditions! "Hey!" I reply, just as surprised. "Wow, do you live here?"

She points to a small tan-colored house down the block. "Right over there. What are you doing here?"

"I'm, um, just waiting for my mom to pick me up."

She looks around behind me, then up and down the street. She must have figured out that I'm out here alone, because she says, "Do you want to wait at my house? You can call her and tell her to pick you up there." Glancing at my purse, she says, "Do you have a cell phone?"

"It's not really working right now."

"You can call from my house then." As we walk, she says, "I never got to really thank you for what you did. I couldn't believe it when I saw you standing on that table! How did you ever think to turn the clock back?"

I smile. "A very smart ten-year-old taught me. She loves to dance, too. I think she'd like to know that she helped."

"Well, I really owe both of you," she says, pushing open her front door. "I never would have made it into the program otherwise."

"You made it! That's great!"

She takes the leash off Bandit and he jumps onto the couch and instantly closes his eyes. "I know! I'm so excited!"

"I'm really happy for you." And I am. Even though I don't know her at all. I redden when I realize I don't even know her *name*.

Just as I open my mouth to ask her, she says, "My name's Sasha, what's yours?"

"Rory," I reply.

We smile kind of awkwardly at each other, and then I look away and glance around the house. It's pretty much the opposite of Natalie's, even though it's only a few houses away. The furniture looks very well lived in. Cardboard boxes line the hallway, and books and toys are scattered around in piles and stacks. "We just moved in last month," she explains. "Still working on unpacking."

"Where did you move from?"

"Up north," she says. "It's very different here. At first it was kind of hard on all of us, but things have gotten better. Hey, I have to finish making dinner. Do you want to come into the kitchen with me? You can call from there."

"Sure." I follow her down the hall, careful not to knock into any of the boxes. She hands me a phone, and I dial Mom's cell.

"Hello?" she says hesitantly. Clearly she doesn't recognize the number.

I quickly fill her in and ask her to pick me up here.

"I don't like the idea of you hanging out at a stranger's house, Rory."

"She's not a stranger. I'm fine, trust me."

"Well, okay. I'm on my way."

I put the phone back on the counter and lean against it. "My mom's a little, uh, overprotective."

Sasha nods knowingly. "My mom's a worrier, too. She told me once she just wants to keep us from getting hurt, you know, because life's not always easy."

I nod. "I've definitely found that out lately."

Sasha starts pulling vegetables out of the refrigerator. I can't help thinking how she seems really young to be making dinner for her whole family. I can't even make coffee!

As if reading my mind, she says, "My brothers and sister and I take turns making dinner. We had to learn really young because my mom usually has to work late. She'll be home on time tonight, though. Our great-aunt is coming."

I watch as she sets the oven to 400 and sticks some potatoes in to bake.

"So," she says, stacking plates on the table. "I guess you were at a party? I mean, you look kind of dressed up."

I look down my dress and blush. "Yeah, I was. My first boy-girl party, actually." Then I blush harder. Why did I say that? I must seem so young and inexperienced to her.

But she just grins and says, "Well, you look very nice. I'm sure a lot of boys noticed."

I shake my head. "Trust me, people don't notice me unless I'm disfigured in some way."

"Are you disfigured a lot?"

"More than you'd think."

She laughs, opens a can of corn, and pours it into a pot on the stove. She turns the burner on, and a flame jumps, then quickly settles down. I've never seen a stove with a real flame before. I wonder if I should volunteer to help, but honestly I'm afraid I'll just mess things up.

"So why do you think people don't notice you?" she asks, stirring the corn as it heats up.

I shrug. "I don't know. It's always been that way. I guess I don't make much of an impression on people."

At that moment, the front door opens and footsteps and laughter fill the front room. Sasha turns the heat off from under the corn. "Come on. I want you to meet my family. I should warn you, there are a lot of them!"

I swing my purse onto my shoulder and follow her out of the kitchen. When we turn the corner into the room, Sasha says, "Everyone, this is Rory. She's the girl who helped me get into the ballet audition!"

Five dark heads and one gray one turn in our direction. All talking instantly halts. "You!" a teenage boy exclaims. "You're the girl with the dollar at the pet store!"

I stare at him, shocked, as the memory floats back to me.

"No!" a younger boy declares, pushing to the front of

the group. "She's the girl who helped me find my class the first day of school when no one else would!"

"Rory found *Green Eggs and Ham* for me!" the littlest boy says.

The grandmother smiles. "This is the young lady who caught Bandit when he got away from me."

Sasha's head is turning from person to person, mouth hanging open, just like mine. Then her mom steps forward. "You helped me get my job at the bookstore."

I stare as recognition slowly dawns. I step backward, almost stumbling, unable to absorb this.

"Rory," a girl's voice utters, cracking with emotion. "Because of you, I got to kiss Jake Harrison when you could have done it yourself. Instead he wound up hitting you in the face with a locker!" Kira throws her arms around me. "I'll never be able to repay you as long as I live, but I'm going to try." It's a good thing she's holding on so tight, because I really might fall right over.

Then everyone starts talking and laughing at once and shaking my hand and formally introducing themselves. "Well, Rory," Sasha says, her eyes bright. "What was that you were saying about not making an impression on people?"

The doorbell rings. "That must be Auntie," Kira says, untangling herself from me and running to the door. She returns a few seconds later, dragging a short, stocky woman with white hair behind her. "Auntie, I want you to meet Rory. Wait till you hear what she did!"

The old woman smiles, a long, slow smile. And when she does, a birthmark shaped like a duck wiggles on her cheek.

Chapter Seventeen

This time I really do stagger backward. Luckily Sasha is standing there to catch me. "It's you!" I exclaim. "How . . . what . . . how . . ."

Sasha leads me over to the couch, which I practically fall into.

"You know Auntie Angelina, too?" Kira says, hurrying to sit next to me. "You must have done something great for her, too, like you did for the rest of us!"

Angelina smiles and sits down in a chair opposite me. "Actually, I was the one to rescue Rory. From a drainpipe, if memory serves."

"You sure get around," Sasha says, shaking her head in wonder.

So many words are trying to tumble out of my mouth

that I can't seem to put them in the right order. Finally I'm able to ask, "What did you mean that day, when you said I wouldn't get what I want until I see what I need?"

"Did I say that?" she says, looking around innocently.

"Auntie!" Sasha's mom admonishes. "You didn't fill this girl's head with any of your crazy predictions, did you?"

"Would I do that?" Angelina asks. Then she winks at me. "I think you already know what I meant, don't you?"

I shake my head and lean back against the cushions. I really *don't* know.

"I'll give you a hint. It's right here in this room."

I sit up again, taking in the shining faces in the room, and I feel like something is starting to wiggle its way into my head.

Angelina continues, "Lots of people can look at a situation, but you *see* it."

"And looking is different than seeing," I hear myself say.

Angelina claps her hands. "Exactly! Truly being able to see the needs of others around you, that is a rare gift. Only when you embrace it will you start to learn who you are, and begin going after what you really want."

"But what do I really want?"

She shrugs. "That's for you to figure out as you go along." She leans forward and whispers, "You're already on your way."

I think about the chance to kiss Jake, and how I gave it to someone else without fighting for it because I couldn't even admit to myself that I didn't feel ready to do it. And then today at the party. Normally I would never have turned away from something I was finally allowed to do, something my friends were doing. But I did. I *did* turn away. And it led me here. How many of the things on my list had I really wanted to do, and how many did I just think I was supposed to do because I was now a certain age? And once I'd done them, how many did I really want to do again? I have a lot to think about.

The doorbell rings and the older boy strides to the door. He returns with my mom. She takes in the scene with a mixture of concern and surprise. I stand up, my legs shaky, but firm.

I take a deep breath. "Mom, this is . . . everyone!"

They all gather around her, talking at once. By the time they get their stories sorted out, Mom looks like *she* needs to sit down, too. "Well! You've certainly been busy, Rory!"

I blush.

"I'd love to hear more about it in the car."

They all make me promise to come back soon and everyone (including Bandit) insists on following us out to the driveway. Something is nagging at me, though, and I can't figure out what it is. Halfway to the car, it hits me, and I stop short. Angelina hadn't heard the stories about everything that had happened. She didn't hear them until *after* my mom showed up. But somehow she knew. She knew before all the others did. I whirl around, but Angelina isn't with us. "I'll be right back," I promise, and dart back into the house.

Angelina is still in her chair, my purse in her outstretched hand. "Forget something?"

Ack! I had totally forgotten about it. Clearly I've got a lot of self-improvement yet to go. I take it from her and clear my throat. "I just wanted to, um, thank you for, you know, *everything*."

She scoffs. "I didn't do anything." Then, with a twinkle, she adds, "Well, except rescue you from the drainpipe. The rest you did by yourself."

"Will I see you again?"

She smiles. "I'm like a bad penny. I keep coming back."

I lean down and kiss her on the cheek. Before she can protest, I run back outside. Sasha's mom holds my car door open for me, and I slide in. They all wave until our car turns the corner at the end of the street.

"Mom, before we talk, can I borrow your cell?"

She grabs it from the cup holder. As she hands it to me, she warns, "I'll be wanting to hear what happened to yours.

You can just tack that on to all the other stories you're about to share. The one about turning back the hands on a clock sounds particularly interesting."

"Okay," I say, hoping that if I can draw out the other stories long enough, we'll arrive at home before I ever get to the part about reaching my arm halfway down someone's toilet.

Annabelle picks up on the first ring. "Mrs. Swenson? What's wrong? Is Rory okay?"

Boy, Annabelle and my mom really DO have a lot in common! "It's me," I tell her. "I'm fine. I just want to ask you something."

"Fire away."

I take a deep breath. "I wanted to ask you why you're friends with me. I mean, like, why you'd want me as your best friend."

She doesn't hesitate before replying. "That's easy. I like myself better when I'm around you. It's like you see into me and I can't hide anything."

I lean into the seat and smile. "Thanks."

"Hey, can you ask your mom if she has a twenty-percent-off coupon for the shoe store on Main Street? I heard they gave them out last week."

I ask and Mom nods.

"Yup, you can have it."

"Cool. I'll call you tonight and tell you about the rest of the party."

"Okay. I'll be home all night."

When I hand her back the phone, Mom says, "I thought tonight was upside-down roller coaster night."

I smile and shake my head. "I was thinking of building a fort instead."

Without taking her eyes off the road, she nods and whispers, almost to herself, "There is more to life than increasing its speed."

Even though I'm pretty sure I heard her, I ask, "What did you say?"

"I didn't say anything. Gandhi did."

"Gandhi? The guy from India? First Dad quotes the Bible, and now you're quoting Gandhi?"

She shrugs and grins. "We're branching out."

I settle back in my seat, feeling like a weight has been lifted off my shoulders. I don't plan to wish for anything for a while. I don't plan to chart out the future, at least not right away. Things are pretty good right now, right where I am.

Maybe Sawyer and Throckmorton would like to join me in the fort.

About the Author

Wendy Mass is the author of the award-winning books for young readers *A Mango-Shaped Space, Leap Day, Jeremy Fink and the Meaning of Life, Heaven Looks a Lot Like the Mall, Every Soul a Star,* and *11 Birthdays.*

She lives with her family in New Jersey. Visit her online at www.wendymass.com.